PRAISE FOR *WHITE LEOPARD*

"Every once in a great while you meet an author who not only talks the talk and walks the walk, but actually writes it right—Laurent Guillaume's *White Leopard* is the perfect combination of street smarts and literary talent."
—Craig Johnson, author of the *Walt Longmire Mysteries*, the basis of the hit Netflix drama *Longmire*

"Fans of classic hard-boiled PI fiction will relish Guillame's first book to be translated into English... He delivers a tale of high-level corruption that will resonate with James Ellroy readers."
—*Publishers Weekly (starred review)*

"This is crime fiction as hard-boiled as it gets. Guillaume, winner of literary prizes in France, is likely to win fans here, too."
—*Booklist*

"West Africa is brought vividly to life in this enthralling, fast-paced noir."
—*Foreword Reviews*

"A powerful novel with keys to understanding what is at play in Mali."
—*Midi Libre*

"Guillaume displays remarkable knowledge about Mali and its underworld."
—*Liberation*

"Guillaume's energetic writing offers readers a hard-boiled mystery set in a Sahel eaten away by corruption."
—*Alibi Magazine*

An intensely true-to-life mystery on steroids. It's raw, authentic and topical."
—*Emotions Literary Blog*

White Leopard

Laurent Guillaume

Translated from French by Sophie Weiner

LE FRENCH BOOK ▮

First published in France as
Black Cocaïne
by Editions Denoël
©2013 Editions Denoël

English translation ©2015 Sophie Weiner
First published in English in 2015
by Le French Book, Inc., New York

http://www.lefrenchbook.com

Translator: Sophie Weiner
Translation editor: Amy Richards
Proofreader: Chris Gage
Cover designer: Jeroen ten Berge

ISBNs:
Trade paperback: 9781939474506
Hardback: 9781939474520
E-book: 9781939474513

To Olivier Marchal, my brother

"An orphan is not a person who has lost his parents,
but someone who has lost hope."
—Bambara proverb

"It's better to be judged by twelve than
carried by six."
—Popular police saying

PROLOGUE

There she is, a metal monster with a tricked-out engine, lying motionless in a chop shop outside the city. She'd been souped up with heavy side panels and a supercharged engine. Perfect for trafficking. It's stinking hot out, but they really should have closed the door of the garage.

Big mistake.

Sweating's better than bleeding.

I check my watch. I don't have much time before the others show up, lights flashing, sirens blaring, and all that crap. I lift the latch and push the gate open. It hardly squeaks. I stay off the gravel driveway and walk through the overgrown yard to avoid being spotted. The makeshift shop looks like it was once a house. Bodies of abandoned cars are rotting away all around it. Waste oil and battery acid are seeping from their guts, making holes in the weeds. The men are there. They're busy taking apart the front of the car. The crushed radiator and bumper have already been ripped off.

It's the watchdog that spots me—a rottweiler mutt with a big muscular chest. His black and wild coat's full of scars, some of them still fresh, no doubt from being forced to fight in basements of the neighboring projects.

Chained to the rusty body of a Renault 11, he leaps up on all fours, baring a steel-jaw trap and yellow fangs.

He gives a muffled growl. From deep inside.

Slowly, I walk closer, bringing my finger to my lips.

"Shush!" I whisper. How pathetic. The dog turns his huge snout toward his masters. When they don't react, the animal starts barking. The men raise their heads. I freeze. They look at each other and come out of the garage, glancing around. No surprise, considering what they're working on. Eddie, the giant, wipes his huge grease-covered mitts on a rag. Steve, the weakling, approaches the animal, who's barking louder now and foaming at the mouth. He leaps toward me with crazed eyes. The dog's chain looks ready to break. The skeleton of the car rises each time the animal jumps.

"Who's the black asshole?" Steve asks.

"Can't you see he's a pig? Fuck!" Eddie shouts.

"I know he's a cop. Why's he alone?"

The animal has gone quiet. With a half-smile, Steve starts unfastening the chain that holds him back.

"Go on, Panzer. It's lunch time."

I'm not scared. I know what I have to do. I open my jacket and slip my hand on my weapon. The freed watchdog rushes toward me. The two brothers howl with laughter, cheering the attack. I draw my gun, thinking I'll never be able to shoot a target moving that fast. But somehow the first bullet hits the rottweiler in the chest, and the second goes right through the head. Never, not even when I worked the anti-gang unit, had I ever pulled off a shot like that. I'd think it's the hand of God, but I don't believe in God anymore. The beast falls at my feet, his eyes glassy and his tongue hanging out.

"Fuck! Panzer!" Steve shrieks.

"See, I told you! He's a pig!" Eddie yells.

Steve starts backing up, his hands open, like he's leading a prayer.

"Officer, we have nothing to do with this. We just fix up old cars…"

Stunned, I head toward them, my gun dangling from my hand. Eddie, the hothead, decides to take control of the situation. He grabs an enormous monkey wrench from a toolbox and dashes at me, brandishing it above his head. I shoot him in the knee. It must hurt worse than I imagine. He falls to the ground, howling like he's possessed. Steve, meanwhile, is blubbering in the back of the garage. He'd never been the braver of the two brothers. I crouch in front of the bumper. It's dented, like the grille. By the license plate, I see a patch of cream-colored linen. I close my eyes and straighten up. I'm feeling a hundred years old and the downers have no effect.

There's blood on the hood.

I head toward Eddie, who's still yowling and rocking himself in a puddle of oil. I pick up the monkey wrench and swing it. I crack his skull. Then I whack him over and over until I lose count. I only stop because of the excruciating pain in my arm. It feels like it's about to come out of the socket. Panting and nauseated, I look at my reflection in the driver's-side mirror of the car they'd been working on. I'm covered in Eddie's blood and bits of his brain. Steve's throwing up in the back of the garage. He lifts his tearful eyes to me as I walk toward him. Remnants of his last meal are dripping from the corner of his mouth. I drop the monkey wrench.

"It wasn't me. It was Eddie," he says.

But I know which of the two was the driver. I make a fist and crack my knuckles.

1

It was a beautiful morning. It must have been about ten o'clock, but it felt like daybreak. She was waiting for me at the top of the outside stairs. I didn't notice her at first. I was too focused on getting up the crumbling concrete steps. I hadn't had a bout of malaria in several weeks, but I still needed to hold onto the rusty handrail like a shriveled old man. Reckless—perhaps suicidal—geckos were dashing between my feet. When I looked up, she was there, standing on the walkway in the intense June sunshine. She was wearing a white dress as light as the first breezes of the Harmattan, the dry wind that sweeps over West Africa in the fall and winter. Her eyes were full of both seriousness and hope. I wiped the thin layer of sweat from my brow and stepped past her, pretending not to take notice. Beautiful women do nothing but cause me trouble, and judging by her looks, this girl would be World War III. I pulled a key from my pocket and approached the door, with its gold plaque trumpeting "Camara Investigations." She moved aside to let me pass.

"Are you Souleymane Camara?" she asked from behind me as I slid the key in the lock.

I opened the door.

"That depends." I turned around to look her in the face.

She was tall—almost my height—and elegant. She was most likely a native of a Maghreb country. I'd have bet Morocco. I could see the outline of her muscled thighs under her gauzy dress. Her leg was just inches from my hand, and it was all I could do to keep myself from reaching out and touching it. Her jet-black hair was pulled back in a tight bun, with a few wisps around her ears. The style wasn't at all unflattering. It highlighted her perfect oval-shaped face and intense dark eyes, which probed me mercilessly. It had been a late night for me, and based on the look of disapproval in her eyes, the excessive activities I had recently been engaging in were blatantly clear. Strangely, it bothered me that she would judge me so harshly.

"That depends on what?" she said.

"That depends on why you're here and whether I owe you money or have caused harm to you or someone close to you."

"And what if that's the case?"

"Take a number and get in line."

"Are there *that* many people?"

"More than I can count."

"I've come to ask for your help, although I'm starting to question whether it's a good idea."

Her tone was cold and revealed a certain level of education. Underneath, there was a melodious Mediterranean singsong in her voice.

I opened the door all the way and motioned her into the office. "Go ahead."

She paused before entering. I pointed to one of the two chairs in front of my desk, the one without the frayed padding and loose frame. I had left my window open, and the hot midmorning heat was already seeping into the room. I glanced at the traffic outside. The street was congested, and the cop at the intersection was trying desperately to maintain order. On the sidewalk, merchants were hassling the passersby, and the beggars were pleading for handouts from drivers stopped at the light.

I closed the window, and the chaos of Bamako subsided. Using my remote, I turned on the AC. The cool air rushed into the room, drying my sweaty back. With a sigh of satisfaction, I sat down in my made-in-China executive chair. I propped my feet on the desk—also from China—and, with a stone face, stared at my female visitor. It was a technique the older cops had taught me when I was still on the force. Always put the other person in an uncomfortable position. Confronted with silence, they'd want to alleviate the tension, fill the time, and perhaps let slip a few helpful insights—things they would have kept to themselves under different circumstances.

But now my efforts were yielding nothing in return. She maintained a polite silence. Finally, I spoke. I cleared my throat and asked, "Well then, what can I do for you, Mrs....?"

"Ms. Tebessi. Farah Tebessi."

She had insisted on the "Ms.," as if it were of great importance to her. That amused me.

"I'm a lawyer, a member of the Paris bar. Perhaps my name rings a bell for you?"

Indeed, the name struck a vague chord in my brain, which was still foggy from too much alcohol. Something I had read in a paper, something that was mentioned on ORTM radio. I rummaged through the mayhem on my desk and extracted an issue of Le Républicain. "Suspected drug trafficker arrested before flight to Paris," a headline blared. And just below that, a readout: "Police say female passenger had 13 kilos of cocaine hidden in luggage."

The article described the impressive effectiveness of the Bamako drug squad bloodhounds. They had neutralized the "dangerous drug-trafficker" just before she boarded her plane. Accompanying the article was a photo: a woman, who appeared to be in her twenties. Distraught and fatigued, she was handcuffed and posed in front of a table with the seized cocaine.

"That's my sister," Farah said. "My little sister, Bahia."

I threw the paper in the wastebasket. The police had been finding coke all over Bamako—by the kilo and by the line.

"I don't see how I can be of help to you. Your sister's fate is sealed."

Farah Tebessi leaned forward with a pained smile on her face, the kind a teacher uses on a kid who's acting too cocky.

"Look, Mr. Camara..."

"Solo... Call me Solo."

"Solo, Bahia is..." Farah hesitated, then continued. "Bahia is your average girl next door. She's in her second year of law school and works part time at an industrial bakery in Val-d'Oise. She's got a young daughter, but the father's gone. She's just getting by, and I assume that makes her the perfect prey for traffickers. There's no way I'm abandoning her. My niece is waiting for her mother. I want to bring her back to France."

"What you want doesn't matter here."

Farah leaned back and sighed. "I'm sure you realize that I didn't set out on this journey without educating myself beforehand. I'm not naïve. I know the local customs. There's always something that can be done."

"I'm curious to hear what that may be."

"I would like you to contact the examining magistrate responsible for this case and offer him something in exchange for my sister's freedom."

I looked at her skeptically while playing nervously with the tagelmust draped around my neck.

"Are you asking me to buy off a judge?"

She let out a scornful little laugh.

"I thought I made myself clear. Don't act all high and mighty. According to what I've heard, buying off people is the national pastime in Mali."

"Who gave you my name?"

She smoothed her dress and locked eyes with me.

"Thanks to my work as a lawyer, I'm in regular contact with the police. I've even become friends with a few. Commander Lefèvre suggested that I speak with you."

Lefèvre—the head of my old drug squad. Pensively, I rubbed the scars on my left hand.

"He told me not to trust my first impressions, that you were a commendable cop back in the day," Farah Tebessi continued. "He said if someone could help me in this country, it would be you. That's why I haven't given up yet."

"Did he tell you how I'm a disaster waiting to happen and that partnering with me can lead to a whole world of trouble?"

She gave me an irritated look. That was clearly a talent of hers.

"Yes, he told me. But I'm not scared—I mean, by what you did."

My throat was feeling as dry as the Sahel. I looked over at the minibar, where my bottle of Scotch was waiting for me. But it was too early. I had to hold out a little longer—until noon, at least.

"I have a saying: in Mali everything's possible and nothing's certain," I replied.

"Okay then, do everything that's possible. I've already said good-bye to certainties."

"How much?" I asked.

"Fifteen thousand euros for the judge, and three thousand for you," she said. That's about ten million in CFA francs for the judge and two million for you, give or take."

"Divide that in half, and it'll be enough. No need to whet any appetites."

She kept staring at me. "For you too?"

"Yes. For me too."

Farah told me she was staying at the Laïco Hotel, just across from the French embassy. We agreed to meet at the same time the following day. She planned to exchange her euros for the African currency at a Malian bank and hand it over to me at our appointment. A branch of the Mali Development Bank was conveniently located near her hotel. I suggested that she have a guard from the bank accompany her to the hotel. She could leave the money in the hotel safe until our meeting. We shook hands, and she left. I remained seated for a moment, looking back at the minibar. A hint of jasmine wafted in the air.

2

I was walking down the Avenue de l'Yser and, as always, felt suffocated by the powerful smells of open sewers, earth, and spices, despite the cool shade of the centuries-old trees, which gave the river district a measure of charm. I had decided to pay a little visit to Hamidou Kansaye, the police commissioner. He happened to be my father's best friend and was the one man who could shed light on Bahia Tebessi's case. Over time, I had learned that in Bamako, things were rarely what they seemed and that going into situations blind could be risky. And so I had decided to ask the best officer in Mali to help me.

I was working my way through a colorful crowd. A woman with sagging breasts was frying banana beignets. Two giggling toddlers with big bellies were waddling around her, their steps not quite steady. In the streets, antique Mercedes taxis, Chinese mopeds, and city vans—*soutramas*—crowded with passengers were jostling for the right of way. It was a happy uproar of horn honking and curses in the Bambara tongue. Making little progress on foot, I hailed a cab. I gave the driver the address of the national police force and slid into the backseat, trying my best to avoid the broken springs. The police headquarters was in the ACI-2000 district, a monstrous growth of modern buildings and immense Stalin-style avenues on the west side of Bamako.

A good half hour later, the taxi dropped me off in front of the drab yellow headquarters. I asked a guard armed with a Kalashnikov to inform the commissioner of my presence. While he walked over to the security post to use the phone, I took a good look at the building. Even though it had been built no more than two years earlier, it had a seventies-style look. Malians were good at putting up new buildings that looked old right from the start. The guard informed me that Kansaye was waiting. He made sure I knew the way and then, without any other formalities, let me go in unescorted and without even a visitor's badge.

I walked into the monumental—and empty—lobby and climbed two flights of stairs before advancing into the hallway to the commissioner's office. In the waiting room, a police officer in a sky-blue uniform was nodding off on a tattered velvet couch. As I shook him awake, I noted his stripes.

"Deputy chief, the commissioner is expecting me. Could you let him know I'm here?"

The man emerged from his lethargic state and looked at me with empty eyes. Finally, he recognized me. He sat up, saluted, and let out a booming, "*Warakalan Jeman*. I'll inform the commissioner."

"White Leopard."

I had solved a few cases that got heavy play from local crime reporters hungry for front-page stories. The hacks loved to give investigators *noms de guerre*. It spiced up their stories. And so I had joined the inner circle of private sleuths and police detectives with zoology-themed nicknames like the "Sparrow Hawk of Mandé" and "Macky the Wildcat." My sudden crime-solving celebrity brought with it certain advantages. I rarely had to wait for anything, I was invited to society gatherings, and my clients were convinced that I possessed magical powers, thanks to my totem. Animism was still very much alive in Mali, even with a majority of the population being Muslim. Deep down, though, I would have preferred staying in the comfortable shadows of anonymity.

I was White Leopard. It has always surprised me that, despite my mixed-race *café au lait* skin, Malians consider me white. In France I was a black dude on the force. It felt like the fate of the multiracial man meant always being opposite to whatever was commonplace. I was perfectly fine with that. I liked to stick out of the crowd.

The uniformed officer knocked on the metal door, and an electric bolt clicked. The deputy chief stuck his head through the opening and announced that I was there. I didn't hear the response, but the officer waved me in. Hamidou Kansaye was standing behind his desk with the receiver of his telephone glued to his ear. He motioned for me to have a seat. Shivering, I complied. The room felt colder than Siberia. The AC was on full blast, as was often the case in the offices and homes of Mali's rich and powerful. The more powerful you were, the colder it was. One of the three cell phones on the leather desk blotter started vibrating like a big beetle. Kansaye brought it to his free ear. Now he was entertaining two conversations at once. He alternated between French and Bambara as he told off both people on the receiving ends. Kansaye had the reputation of being irascible. His pals on the force had nicknamed him Pinochet. The locals called him "The Incorruptible." I didn't know if that was accurate, but I did know that everyone respected and feared him. Anyone who had ever tried to slip one by him always regretted it. Kansaye never forgot.

He might as well have had "revenge is sweet" sown on a throw pillow.

Finally, he cut the two conversations off, hanging up the fixed phone and wearily throwing the cell on his desk.

After a bit of small talk, he got to the point. "Leopard, to what do I owe this visit?"

Kansaye, a Dogon, was in his sixties, but was still sturdy and vigorous. He had a harsh face and a thin mustache. He was wearing one of the sky-blue boubou robes that he loved. His eyes sparkled, reflecting the keen mind of someone who came from the earth and ancestral traditions. He was also a scholar and a lover of French literature. My father and he were like brothers. So much so that after my father's death, Kansaye felt compelled to watch over me, and God knows he had his work cut out.

"Commissioner, I've come to talk to you about that French woman who was arrested for transporting cocaine."

The commissioner froze and stared at me. I had aroused his interest, which was no easy task.

"How does that concern you?"

"I need to know which examining magistrate has been assigned the case."

His eyes froze on me.

"Why?"

There was no point in procrastinating. I decided to lay my cards on the table. Kansaye had always been a faithful ally. Besides, it was impossible to put anything past this man.

"The mule's sister hired me. She wants me to contact the judge and buy him off."

He stood up and walked over to the AC. The temperature fell from Siberia cold to polar blast.

"How much?"

"Five million."

He shook his head.

"You have to be careful where you step, Solo. This case is more complicated than it seems. Some high-ranking players are involved. I'm walking on eggshells."

"Will you let me talk to Bahia Tebessi?"

He shrugged. "If you insist. She's still being detained by the drug squad. And as for your judge, his name is Moussa Guino. He's an asshole, but a greedy asshole."

Kansaye had just given me the go-ahead.

"*Insha'Allah*," he said in response to my promise to return the favor.

I thanked him and took off.

3

By the time I left the police headquarters, the sun had run half its course. My stomach was growling, and my throat was dry, so I stopped for lunch at Café du Fleuve. I ordered the grilled Nile perch—a West African favorite known as *capitaine*—and a fruit salad, which I enjoyed with three refreshing Flags, a local brew. Because my destination wasn't too far away, I decided to walk there after my lunch. As I passed through a neighborhood filled with small appliance shops, several street peddlers recognized me and invited me to have tea with them under the mango trees. I had some time to kill and accepted. It was an opportunity to practice my shaky Bambara.

After thanking my hosts, I set out for the small red-dirt square bordered by four worn buildings that housed the services under the Ministry of the Interior—national police offices, the juvenile crimes division, the drug squad, and the bureau of investigations. These units were in old villas that were in need of a good paint job. A throng of vendors and the loved ones of prisoners and victims were crowding the entrances. I elbowed my way through and presented myself at the drug squad station.

Three police officers were slouched in woven plastic chairs. Chatting and drinking tea, they pretended to ignore me, and I had to interrupt their conversation to ask them to inform Bagayoko, the chief investigator, of my presence. One of them stood up with a sigh and made a call while giving me sideways glances. I was almost touched by their attempt to make me feel unwelcome. Cops saw me as a poacher, and my celebrity in the eyes of Bamako's citizens made them furious. It's worth noting that the police of Mali aren't very popular. The officer shelled out an "on your orders, Chief" and a "yes, Chief" and hung up. He nodded, indicating I could go in, and sat back down with his colleagues, who were now staring daggers at me.

I found myself in the interior courtyard. A ram and two scraggy sheep were grazing on the brown grass under an old mango tree. I approached the villa, knocked twice on the wrought-iron door, and entered without waiting for a response.

A cold capable of freezing the toughest Antarctic penguins enveloped me. The AC was on turbo. With goose bumps on my arms, I greeted Inspector Bagayoko, thinking about my chances of catching pneumonia at this rate. He was an average-sized man with an average mustache and a below-average intelligence. His ego, on the other hand, was stratospheric, which was confirmed by the framed photos on the wall behind him. They showed him alongside the police commissioner, the prime minister, and even President Amadou Toumani Touré, known as ATT. Bagayoko looked at me smugly from behind his immense desk while I sat down on a chair that had seen better days. I should mention that the man avoided work like the plague. He delegated everything he could to his subordinates so he could indulge in his favorite vice—online poker.

"Hello, Mr. Camara. What's brought you here?"

"Chief, you haven't received a call from Kansaye?" I said, adopting an appropriate look of surprise.

He put on a show of remembering.

"Ah, yes! The commissioner did, indeed, contact me earlier. You're interested in information concerning the Bahia Tebessi investigation."

He leaned forward and slid a sheet of smudged paper to my side of the desk. A few notes that I would have been hard-pressed to decode were scribbled on it.

"Here's what I can tell you. An investigation is under way. It would be kind of you not to divulge this information," he said with a smirk.

I didn't give into his game. He was obviously enjoying the playful farce he was putting on for me. And so we continued staring at each other. He shifted his weight, and his fake leather chair creaked.

"You're not taking the paper?" he asked with a tinge of hostility in his voice.

"There must have been a mistake. I requested a chat with Ms. Tebessi in person," I answered with a contemptuous smile.

"That's out of the question! We're working within the confines of an official investigation. You are familiar with the required confidentiality, aren't you?"

"Nope," I sneered, aware that he probably had already sold the information in his possession to the local media, Radio France Internationale, and the BBC.

I stood up, saluted the chief, and left to enter the early afternoon inferno. Damned heat. I was instantly covered with a thin layer of perspiration. As I called the commissioner, I wondered how many times in a single day I could break a sweat. Fifteen, maybe twenty? When Kansaye picked up, I told him I had hit a dead-end.

"Bagayoko's an idiot. I'll call him immediately."

I lit a cigarillo and waited in the shade of a mango tree.

~ ~ ~

Bagayoko must have gotten a real lashing, because in the next few minutes, the guard-turned-bootlicker, his keys jangling in his hand, was inviting me to follow him. He took me to the "custody facilities," which was what the cops called them. These basic structures were outside the villa and in a small courtyard behind the drug-squad building. With their bare cinder-block walls and rust-bitten bars, they looked more like animal cages than jail cells. The inmates at the Bamako zoo, which was considered a sort of animal hospice, had better accommodations.

A few weary prisoners, slumped against the bars, stared at me with gloomy interest as bugs swarmed around their faces. Bahia Tebessi was sprawled on a scrawny straw mattress on the dusty concrete floor. In the back, a funky smell emanated from the Turkish toilet. It wasn't hard to imagine the young woman's lack of privacy from the guards and her fellow prisoners. She sat up and with difficulty stretched her stiff limbs. Then she rose to her feet and walked over to me. The guard offered to bring me a plastic chair, but I declined. He dragged his flip-flops in the dirt as he walked away.

"Who are you?" Bahia asked.

For two weeks, she had been rotting in this hellhole, plagued by flies during the day, mosquitoes at night, and a constant oppressive heat. Actually, I didn't think her face looked that bad, considering the circumstances.

"Ms. Tebessi, my name is Solo. Your sister has hired me to get you out of here."

"Farah told me about you. She comes to see me every day."

Her weak voice was almost a whisper as she fiddled with the neckline of her filthy T-shirt. She looked like a petite version of her pretty older sister. Her sleep-deprived eyes brimmed with tears. A woman's tears always affect me.

"If I understand correctly, you're my savior?"

"If you say so," I said. "But before we do anything, I need to know more about you and what happened."

She didn't respond right away. "I've already told the police everything," she finally said. "Is this really necessary?"

"Imperative. Go on. I'm listening."

She took a breath and dived into it. "Two months ago, I met a guy in the metro. Some dude from my neighborhood."

"What neighborhood?"

"La Cité des Musiciens in Argenteuil. You know, not far from Paris."

I nodded, indicating that I wanted her to continue.

"He knew I was in a bind, that my boyfriend had split and left me with Samia and no dough. Samia's my daughter. I was working so hard, but I couldn't get out of the hole I was in. After rent, my commute, my babysitter... I needed money. I couldn't hold on much longer."

"Why didn't you ask your parents or sister for help?"

Right away, I regretted the question. She tensed up.

"I have my pride," she said, her eyes gleaming.

For a fraction of a second, I had discerned a ferocious sense of honor in this dirty young woman with tangled hair. I kept myself from pointing out that her pride was now costing her supreme humiliation. It was a weakness I understood.

"It's none of my business, anyway," I said, continuing with my questions. "What was his name—the guy from the metro?"

"I only knew his first name. Demba. He said I could earn a few thousand euros without any risk. I'd go to Mali for free, spend a week in an all-expenses-paid luxury hotel, and wait for his partner to contact me with instructions on bringing back contraband gold in my suitcases. He said there'd be no risk of getting caught, because his friends in Mali bankrolled the cops. Once back in France, I was supposed to meet him at a motel in Seine-et-Marne and hand over the package."

She was getting agitated. Her features were twitching.

"Last month, they gave me my plane ticket to Bamako. When the plane landed, a guy who said his name was Sinaly was waiting for me. He helped me get my overnight bag, slipped me some cash, and took me to the Hotel Olympe in a big black SUV."

I knew the hotel. It sat atop a hill overlooking the lush waters of the Niger. The Economic Community of West African States was on the same avenue. The Hotel Olympe was a huge place, and despite the Soviet-style architecture, it was once luxurious. Now it was no more than a shabby shell of its former self.

"I stayed there for a couple weeks, and Sinaly got back in touch with me," Bahia said.

"What did you do in the meantime?" I asked, cutting her off.

The way she skipped over how she had spent her time seemed suspicious to me.

"I... I had fun with the money that Sinaly gave me. Pools, clubs, stuff I can't afford to do at home."

I nodded. "Okay, go on."

"Sinaly called me late Thursday afternoon on the prepaid cell he had given me. He told me to be ready to fly home that night. He wanted me to leave my overnight bag at the hotel because he intended to switch it out for a bag with gold inside. He'd meet me at the airport and give me that bag. But I didn't want to leave anything at the hotel. I had packed souvenirs for Samia. Sinaly told me that if I didn't do what he said, someone would rip out my guts. He said I wasn't in my country, and I didn't know the rules here. So I did what he told me to do. I left my bag and met him at the airport. He gave me the other one, which I handed over to the airline personnel at check-in. When I went through security, the cops were waiting for me—with the bag. That's when I found out it wasn't gold that I was supposed to take to France."

I pulled a pack of cigarettes out of my pocket and offered her a smoke. She nodded, saying she could really use one. As I held the lighter up for her, she grabbed my hands.

"Farah told me Samia's crying for me. Get me out of here, Mr. Camara," she pleaded, her eyes filling with tears. "I won't be able to make it much longer."

"I'll do everything I can."

4

Moussa Guino was young, thirty at the most. He was wearing an impeccably tailored Western suit. With his arms crossed over his already bulging belly, he assessed me from behind a pair of designer shades whose real purpose, I suspected, was giving him the confidence that he lacked. He most likely belonged to one of those rich Bamako families that had no problem paying for high-level favors or buying their way into cushy government jobs. I was sure he already dreamed of being district attorney, or even the attorney general.

"So just like that, you're representing Bahia Tebessi," he said somewhat distrustfully.

"Exactly, Your Honor. And I have to say I'm impressed," I replied, flashing my most radiant grin.

"How so?"

Now was the time to butter him up. "I have a confession to make. Before our meeting, I asked around about you."

"Oh yeah? And what did you learn?" he asked.

I leaned toward him. "You graduated from Assas University in Paris with an excellent academic record."

Actually, Kansaye had told me that Guino was a mediocre student who had passed only with the help of a diplomatic request from the chancellery.

"People speak of you with great respect," I continued. "There are some who even think you'll be working as a top government official in a few years."

He straightened his shoulders and waved off the compliment.

"You're getting ahead of yourself, Mr. Camara."

I pretended to look puzzled. "At any rate, I was wondering…"

"Yes?"

"Why would such a gifted student choose a humble, although honorable career as a judge when he could have put his immeasurable talents to good use in a corporate position offering loads of money?"

I thought I might be laying it on too thick. But my flattery didn't seem to arouse any suspicions. Just the opposite. Moussa Guino settled more comfortably in his chair. He placed his elbows on his desk and clasped his hands.

"You see, Mr. Camara…"

He paused, searching, I figured, for the perfect words.

"Serving our country requires sacrifices. But I love Mali, and I want to return what it has given me. It's like a son honoring his mother for giving him life-sustaining milk."

I was speechless for several seconds. When it came to laying it on, Guino was using mudbrick plaster, compared with my thinned-out paint.

"That's beautiful and so true," I said, wishing I could shed a tear for effect.

"Thanks. Now getting back to our case, I won't pretend that it hasn't gotten off to a rough start."

"I don't doubt it," I agreed.

"The evidence is irrefutable. I'd even say it's conclusive."

"Indeed, indeed. But I imagine that a man of your importance doesn't usually waste his precious time on investigations involving insignificant drug mules."

"I intend to follow this case all the way to the brains behind the sordid affair," he said, raising his voice.

"Your Honor, we both know that the bosses of these drug-smuggling networks keep all the players isolated from each other. I doubt that Bahia Tebessi could tell you any more than what she's already said to the police. If you rely too heavily on her story, you'll get nowhere, and you'll risk disappointing your superiors."

Guino looked worried. As I expected, he hadn't thought much about the problem. He was too busy licking the boots of those higher up in his chain of command.

"What do you suggest then?"

I pointed to the ancient computer loafing on his desk.

"Bahia Tebessi's family is prepared to donate a substantial sum to this country's judicial system if it agrees to act benevolently toward this case. You'd be able to replace your device from the Middle Ages, for example."

I held my breath.

"How much would this donation amount to?"

The fish had taken the bait. Now for a bit of skillful maneuvering...

"Two million. The family has humble origins."

He raised his eyes to the ceiling.

"What do you expect me to do with such a measly sum? You can see our miserable working conditions. Tell your client that this matter would cost the family much more in legal fees."

I pretended to think things over and tried to look vexed. "We'd be willing to go up to three million, but no more than that."

Moussa Guino paused. "Four million. That's the least I'll accept. Don't forget, I'll have to justify dismissing the case. It won't be easy, considering all the attention her arrest has gotten."

I gave him a sympathetic smile. Getting his superiors to swallow this bitter pill would mean that he'd have to fork over some money too. I stood up and pulled my cell out of my pocket. I couldn't cede too quickly.

"I'll call my clients and try to persuade them."

He nodded and I left his office. Once in the courtyard of the Commune III district courthouse, I put the phone to my ear and continued the farce while I smoked a cigarillo, quite pleased with myself. Once it was finished, I returned to Moussa Guino's office.

"It's a go. They've accepted the deal."

We shook hands and finalized the logistics of handing over the money, which would take place before noon the next day.

"I congratulate you, Your Honor, for your self-sacrifice and sense of public service," I told him as I left his office.

5

I think about them all the time. It's stupid. When they were alive, I never thought about them enough. My life was miserable. I was working day and night. The chases, the arrests, the adrenaline, all that bullshit. The other narcs and I, we thought we were the only ones living like that. We thought we were in a league of our own outside the society we protected. So we took some liberties. It was only normal. We had our share of fun, all right: booze, drugs, whores, seedy motels and sweaty sheets, bloodshot eyes and hangover mouths. The next morning, her eyes would look heavy and wounded, while I'd stare at the floor.

In reality, I was the one who killed them—never being there, never doing anything the way it should've been done, thinking only about myself. She wanted to fly to the moon. I didn't. My life was that piece-of-shit job. Now I'm lugging around my guilt like a suitcase I can't get rid of. Sometimes I can forget about the throbbing pain, but it's always lurking. It keeps me from burying them once and for all.

It's my punishment.

This morning, for the first time, I was hardly thinking about them. I had a meeting with Farah Tebessi. When

I showed up at the Laïco Hotel, she was sipping juice by the pool, wearing pumps and a khaki dress that hugged her elegant silhouette. My father liked to say that shoes revealed everything about a woman's personality. What *these* shoes revealed had me wiping the drool off the corner of my mouth. As we shook hands, a waiter came over. I ordered what she was drinking, even though I would have preferred something with more of a kick. She didn't want to discuss my negotiations with Guino or the money I had saved her. We chatted for a few minutes, and she handed over the payoff for Guino and half of my fee. She reassured me that she'd be giving me the rest as soon as her sister was freed. That wasn't what we had agreed on, but I didn't care. I could sense that she wanted to cut our encounter short and that the stories of corruption in Mali—now that her problems were almost solved—were weighing heavily on her. I figured I'd have another opportunity to see her again. So I got up and said good-bye.

Later that day, I gave Moussa Guino his money. I waited a good fifteen minutes as he painstakingly counted the bills to make sure it was all there. Once he was satisfied, he thanked me cordially, and we parted on good terms.

I returned to my office to tackle overdue paperwork before meeting with a new client: a rather large woman who came in wheezing after her climb up the outside stairs. She smelled like sweat and patchouli, and I had to restrain myself from cracking open a window. As she noisily blew her nose into a tissue, she asked me to check on her husband, a rich businessman. Some of their mutual friends had told her that he intended to take a second wife—a younger, thinner, more fertile woman was already his mistress. The woman's blubbering was giving me a headache, and after she left I poured myself a glass of Scotch and then another, as my skull was still pounding. My new client had deposited a wad of oily bills on my desk, even though I hadn't asked for an advance. Long after she was gone, I stared at the money, not having the energy to actually count it.

I spent the last part of the afternoon tailing the husband but didn't learn anything the wife hadn't already told me. I decided to go home. I live in the residential neighborhood of Badalabougou on the right bank of the river. When my dad died four years ago, he left me his house on Rue Thirteen and a nice sum of money that keeps me comfortable. It's a charming structure, although during flood season it occasionally gets wet. The house and the money are all that's left of the old man's wealth. My half-brothers and half-sisters long ago squandered the rest.

My dad had met my mom in the seventies, when he was a student in France. She was a bourgeois Parisian from the sixth arrondissement. Their relationship caused quite a few disagreements in their respective families, especially my mother's. At the time, their marriage was said to be against nature. What a term that was. After their initial passion cooled, their cultural differences were all that remained. There was constant cheating on one side and glacial distrust on the other. Bamako was the last straw. My father made it a point to return as frequently as possible, while my mother abhorred the "vile city that stank like an open sewer." On top of that, he sent a large amount of money made during his career as a French commercial banker to the country she detested. They split up and then played tug-of-war over me from their respective homes—Africa and Europe, Third World and First World, black and white. My father remarried and had a bunch of kids at a ripe old age, while my mother sank into bitter resentment. They still loved each other, but their differences won out. For both of them, I represented their dashed dreams. When a relationship is cross-cultural—and especially interracial, as we stupidly call it—one person always has to make a sacrifice by giving up their heritage. My heritage was at the end of a dirt road.

I honked, and Drissa, my *gardinier*—that's what Bamako residents call someone who tends the grounds and garden—opened the gate to let in my old Toyota Land Cruiser, which my father had also left me. He opened the squeaky driver's-side door and gave me a warm welcome.

"Evening, boss. How was your day?" he asked, as he had every evening for years.

I replied with the usual "it went well," and after looking through the mail, I took a seat on my patio, which faced the river. Meanwhile, Drissa prepared two glasses of Scotch in the living room. I opened my box of cigars on the small rattan table and took out a Cuban robusto that a Lebanese client had given me as a thank-you for a service I had provided. I heard ice cubes clink as I lit the cigar. I waved the match to put it out and took a puff of the rich, lush tobacco. Drissa came back, carefully carrying the filled-to-the-rim glasses. He was more than sixty years old. His eyesight was declining, and his hands trembled from a lifetime spent drinking—even though he was Muslim—but he never spilled a drop of my Scotch. Drissa had principles. I loved his weathered-like-old-leather face, his watery eyes, and his white wooly hair, which attracted blades of cilantro and basil when he cooked. I had encouraged him to retire on several occasions, but he stubbornly refused, often asserting that he had served my father before me, and he would serve my son when the time came. I didn't get upset with him about that. He didn't know the pain it reawakened in me. I understood that nothing was awaiting him outside this home. His family lived in Burkina Faso and had forgotten him long ago. He would die the day he was no longer of service to anyone. So we took care of each other.

He sat down beside me and lit a contraband cigarette. After clinking our glasses, we drank in silence.

By the water, fishermen were casting their nets. Upriver, the sun was disappearing in a bed of unlikely colors.

I sure do love a good sunset.

6

Deep in dreamland, I felt someone shake me. I groaned and buried my head in the pillow. They shook me again.

"Boss, wake up!"

I recognized Drissa's voice.

"What the hell is going on?" I grumbled. My eyes were pasty, and I had a nasty taste in my mouth. Drissa was standing there in his briefs and a stained undershirt that was full of holes.

"It's the police. They're asking for you!"

I sat up. My alarm clock read 5:39. I sighed, got out of bed, and stumbled over to the chair where I had thrown my boxers and T-shirt.

A guy in a sky-blue uniform was waiting by the gate. He was standing in front of a pickup that had "*Police nationale—commissariat du 7e arrondissement*" painted on it. The paint job was drippy. I introduced myself, still half asleep and in my underwear. He didn't seem bothered by that.

"The commissioner has requested your services, *Warakalan Jeman*," he said.

He refused to provide any more information. Annoyed, I took a lightning-fast shower while Drissa prepared my coffee. I put on the same clothes I had worn the day before, wrapped my tagelmust around my neck, and quickly gulped my beverage. It was thick and black like gasoline, but honestly tasted much grosser. With my faculties nearly restored, I joined the police officer. We rode in silence. After crossing the Martyrs Bridge, we went through the Niarela neighborhood. Traffic was still light, but the sun was already sizzling in the cloudless sky. It was going to be a stifling day, I mused while yawning. I wondered what Kansaye wanted from me. He wasn't known for being an early bird, and the case had to be awfully important for the powerful police commissioner to show up at a crime scene in person. At least that was my impression of things. I was starting to feel an omen-like gnawing in my gut.

Through the Toyota pickup's grimy window, I saw women doing their ablutions in the gutters and guys brushing their teeth with whistling thorn branches. Busted-up heavy-goods vehicles were parked along the street in the industrial part of Bamako. Drivers were sleeping in their ancient trucks because they were allowed to drive in the capital only at night, when traffic was lighter. At last, we arrived in the Sotuba neighborhood. My official chauffeur parked the pickup in front of an agricultural center, beside two navy blue police vehicles and a white Renault Laguna coupe, which I recognized as belonging to the criminal investigations unit, formally known as homicide. Officers were dozing in the front seats of their vehicles. My driver laconically indicated a small group of people along the riverbank, then leaned back in his seat and closed his eyes. Fractions of a second later he was snoring.

To meet up with the other cops, I needed to cross an industrial wasteland with tall weeds that made me incredibly nervous. I was afraid of sneaky reptiles hiding in the grass. The riverbanks were infested with snakes, most of which were poisonous. I hated those creatures. Not a soul could convince me that God had anything to do with their creation. So I advanced with caution. I batted down the brush and placed my foot down only when I was absolutely sure no scaly beasts were slithering beneath.

Dressed in his light blue boubou, Kansaye was conversing with one of his associates, Pierre Diawara, a tall friendly-faced guy in his fifties, who was wearing a light short-sleeved shirt and khaki slacks. Pierre, the chief inspector with the criminal investigations unit, was listening to Kansaye, but when he spotted me, his face lit up. Kansaye followed his gaze.

"Finally, you're here," Kansaye said, glaring at me. "Was it that hard getting your toubab ass out of bed?"

I saluted him ceremoniously, and Kansaye twitched as he picked up the sarcasm beneath my formal groveling. I turned to Pierre and gave him a hug. Over the years, he had become one of my few true friends in Bamako.

"Commissioner, to what do I owe the pleasure of being brought here at the crack of dawn?"

"Quit being a jackass, Solo." Looking at Pierre he said, "Show him, Diawara."

Taking me by the arm, the chief inspector led me to the riverbank.

He didn't have to point. I saw it. She was bobbing in the waters of the Djoliba—the Mandinka people's name for the Niger—her hair rippling gently in the water and her wide eyes fixed in an expression of unspeakable surprise.

Bahia Tebessi.

The submerged branch of a river shrub was holding her up at the armpit. Her throat had been slit so brutally, her spine was all that held her head on. She was naked, and her dead white skin looked like an obscene glob on the dark water. Rising bile burned my esophagus. I had to look away. I turned my eyes toward the skeleton of

Bamako's third bridge, which was under construction up-river. Dozens of Chinese workmen were scurrying over it like ants. She had probably been thrown in from there.

"She must have known more than we thought."

Kansaye was standing next to me, his face inscrutable.

"It certainly looks like she did," I answered, feeling bone weary.

"That was your client?"

"No, her sister was my client. A lawyer from Paris."

He nodded and said nothing for a moment. "I tried to get hold of you," he finally said. "Do you ever answer your phone?"

I took my cell out of my jacket pocket, where it had spent the night. I had a dozen missed calls. All from Kansaye and Farah Tebessi.

"Has anyone contacted her sister?" I asked.

~ ~ ~

She got out of the cab. Her face was red and puffy. She took hesitant steps, glancing around with distraught eyes. They went right through me, as though I wasn't there. The cops had stopped what they were doing and were staring at her. I started walking toward her just as she caught sight of her sister's body on a stretcher, covered with a damp sheet. Some men were carrying it to an old black Mercedes station wagon. I caught her as she began running toward them and took her in my arms. She tried to pull away but finally slid to the ground, shaking with silent sobs. I crouched down and held her face in my hands.

"I know what you're feeling right now."

She looked at me with a tormented expression.

"What am I going to tell my parents? What am I going to tell Samia?"

"Come on. Let's get out of here," I said as I helped her to her feet.

7

We made our way back to the main road and were lucky enough to hail a roaming cab—an old yellow Mercedes 190, like the thousands of other cabs in Bamako. I gave the sleepy driver an address, and after a short ride, he dropped us off at the Hotel Mande in the Niger neighborhood. In another lifetime, this place was a jewel of the Malian hotel industry, but the years had not been kind. Vestiges of the hotel's former glory were peeking through the layers of cheap paint. I guided Farah Tebessi across the lobby to the patio, which rested on pilings. Just below, I could hear the Djoliba's lapping waters. Bozo fishermen with muscled arms were paddling upstream to their fishing spots. An apathetic waiter walked over to us, and I ordered two coffees. Farah remained hopelessly mute.

"I tried calling you last night," she said at last, her voice hoarse.

"I know."

Before she could say anything else, the waiter returned with our order. He placed the coffees on the table and slipped away.

"I was supposed to pick Bahia up at the drug unit last night..."

Her voice faded. Tears streamed down her face and dropped off her chin. But she did nothing to wipe them away.

"The police told me that she had already left. That she had taken a taxi—without waiting for me. Why would she do that?"

I swallowed my coffee. Disgusting.

"What are you going to do now?" I asked.

"I'll call my parents, then handle the formalities," she said with absent eyes. "They'll want to bury her in France."

"If there's anything I can do to help, please let me know."

She stirred her coffee without taking a sip.

"Yes, there is something you could do."

"I'm listening."

"I want you to track down the people who did this to my sister and kill them," she said. "All of them." She banged down her spoon and balled her napkin in her hand.

I didn't react, just stared at the river, where kids were lathering up and shrieking happily.

"I don't do that."

"You've done it before. Do it again," she said, clearly trying to control her venomous rage.

"No."

"I'll pay you. I'll give you lots of money."

I stood up and threw a two-thousand-franc bill on the table.

"That's not what happened. I'm not a murderer."

I turned and left, and from behind me I heard a hysterical voice. "Yes you are! It's in your blood!"

8

She called me a good twenty times in the following days, but I wouldn't allow myself to answer. The calls stopped on the fourth day. I surrendered to the routine of my investigations. More specifically, I tackled my case involving the insensitive husband who allegedly wanted to take a second wife. I quickly identified the mistress: his secretary. I have to admit the young woman was spectacular. She could make celibates drool with lust. Obviously, she wasn't hired for her typing skills. I succeeded in spotting them together in a *maquis*, one of those bars where lovers feel free to express themselves. I sat down at a table next to theirs, ordered a Castel, and while pretending to send a text message took their picture. The image was blurry, but you could make out enough to understand the true nature of their relationship. With my eyes glued to the screen, I eavesdropped. I learned the young woman's name was Aïssata, and she was from the Ivory Coast.

Satisfied, I finished my beer, got up, and left the bar. Once outside, I checked my watch. It was seven thirty. I called Drissa to tell him not to wait up, then got in my old Toyota. I was hungry. I decided to go eat at Milo's pizzeria and knock back a few glasses of Scotch with him.

Chez Milo was on a dirt road in the Niarela neighborhood. As I was parking along the cracked wall of the pizza
place, a crippled man with a makeshift crutch came up to
my car and used hand gestures to guide my maneuvering.
When I got out and shut the creaky door, he greeted me
enthusiastically.

"Good evening, boss. Want me to keep an eye on your
car?"

I glanced at my dented heap of junk. "You really think
it's worth the trouble?"

"I really do. It's a nice car. None better in all of Mali,"
he said cheekily.

I said okay, and as I entered the pizzeria, he gave me
a friendly wave to reassure me of his vigilance. I walked
through the restaurant and out to the terrace, where half
a dozen couples were dining. Heating coils, whose smoke
was meant to shoo away the mosquitoes, were burning
near the tables. Milo was sitting at the outside bar, sipping
a Jack Daniels and telling off his head chef, as he often did.

"Fuck! How did I get saddled with a cook like you? Pay
a little attention, dammit! Pizzas deserve our respect."

I sat down next to him.

"Hey, Camara. The usual?" he asked, extending his
large paw, which I shook.

I handed him my pack of cigarillos. He helped himself,
and we lit our little cigars with the flame of my Zippo.
According to legend, the Serb had served ten years in the
French Foreign Legion as a nurse or a sharpshooter. I didn't
really know which. He never talked about it, even when
he got drunk, which happened a lot.

Milo Stojakovic was not a very tall guy—five feet sev-
en at the most. His broad shoulders and thick forearms
bulging underneath one of the dreadful Hawaiian shirts
he had a habit of wearing discouraged even the rowdiest

customer looking for a fight. But the most impressive thing about him was his intense blue eyes in a large face with deep wrinkles. You could see an animalistic violence in him. I had been his friend for years, but he could still give me the jitters. No one knew how long he had been knocking around in Africa, and no one even knew his actual age. If I had to guess, I would have said anywhere between forty-five and sixty.

A waitress placed a Macallan, neat, and an ashtray in front of me. Milo had some Lebanese pals who provided him with stuff that was hard to find in this country, like good single malt. I savored a sip of the nectar. So there we sat, enjoying our drinks and smokes.

"You eating with me?" he asked eventually, putting out the smoking butt of his cigarillo.

The waitress seated us beneath an arbor. Silently, we ate our two four-seasons pizzas—olives for summer, mushrooms for fall, prosciutto for winter, and artichokes for spring—while gazing at the Bamako sky. At the end of the meal, he presented two Cohiba Esplendidos acquired from Cuban friends who worked at the Gabriel Touré Hospital. You could definitely say that Milo Stojakovic had a solid network of suppliers.

We smoked and drank our whiskeys, which the waitress had replenished. By the time I left, I was staggering a bit and feeling pretty good. When I walked up to my car, the man with a crutch joined me and held out his hand. Feeling charitable, I gave him a thousand-franc bill. He smiled and held the door as I got into my vehicle. I was about to start the engine when he tapped the hood.

"Boss, I don't know if this is important..."

"Say it anyway," I instructed.

"When you got here, there were two guys in an SUV behind you, a black Land Cruiser."

I felt my heart beating faster.

"Where are they now?"

"Still there, on the street."

"What do they look like? Are they toubabs?"

He shook his head.

"No, they're *falafi*."

They were black. I glanced in the rearview and spotted the Land Cruiser, whose shiny exterior glistened in the light of an old rusty streetlamp. Not very subtle. I couldn't get a look inside because of the lamp's reflection on the windshield. I thanked my informant with the crutch and slipped him a second bill—a two-thousand bill this time. As I turned the key, the Land Cruiser's headlight went on. I pulled out, and the Land Cruiser pulled out behind me.

9

I was driving on Route Koulikoro with one eye glued to the rearview. The Land Cruiser was on my ass. By now I could easily make out the two silhouettes in the front seat. Either the driver didn't know rule No. 1—leave some room between you and the target—or he was taunting me. The latter was a bigger cause to worry. This wasn't the first time I'd been tailed. In my field, making enemies is inevitable. People have always tried to intimidate me. Generally, I take a philosophical approach. But on this night I wasn't in the mood. I decided to get rid of the two assholes. Given the difference in power between our two vehicles, I'd have to ask for help. At the intersection of Marne and Modibo-Keïta avenues, three traffic cops were dozing on their Chinese mopeds. I parked close to them, and from the corner of my eye, I saw the Land Cruiser do the same about two hundred feet back. I motioned to the officers and lowered my window. The older one, and therefore higher in rank, raised an eyebrow. Grumbling, he walked over to my car. He bent down to my window and asked what I wanted. He didn't recognize me, which worked to my advantage.

"Sergeant, I don't mean to bother you, but there's a strong possibility that I'm in danger."

He looked at me dubiously. "We're here to help our citizens," he said.

I didn't pick up much conviction in his voice. But the ten-thousand-franc bill disappeared like magic when I slipped it in his hand.

"You have my full attention," he said. Now there was a lot of conviction in his voice.

"You see that big SUV parked just behind us and the two guys inside?"

He glanced at the Land Cruiser and nodded.

"They're hired muscle that my associate has sent after me. He wants my share of our company and is willing to do anything for it, even use extreme measures."

"What exactly do you want us to do?" the cop asked.

"I want you to hold them back long enough for me get somewhere safe."

"No problem."

He turned toward the two other officers and barked orders in Bambara. They then got up and headed toward the Land Cruiser with their hands on their ancient Tokarev pistols. The higher rank smiled at me and tapped the hood of my car.

"Go ahead. We'll take care of them."

I started the engine and sped away as fast as my old Toyota would allow. The cops weren't going to wait too long before doubling down.

I made it home without any incidents and got into bed feeling deeply alone. For once, I experienced a relatively calm sleep. My nightmares had dispersed. They, too, needed to breathe. The next day I went to my office. I had an appointment with the cheated-on wife, and I didn't even have time to make my coffee before she burst in and collapsed in the chair in front of my desk, breathing as heavily as an ironworker. When I showed her the photos of her husband canoodling with his mistress, she whimpered and then began wailing. Her blubbery chest and gelatinous thighs bounced with each sob. Even with the aspirin I took as a precaution, I felt a migraine looming.

"I hope his cock rots inside that slut's dirty twat, and she shrivels up and dies after getting eaten by rabid dogs."

She calmed down when I told her that the object of her husband's passion was Ivorian. Because her husband's family had lived in Bamako for generations, he would never take a foreigner as a second wife. Now my client didn't feel threatened. Instantly, her sniveling stopped.

"At any rate, I'm going to have a little chat with him. This isn't seemly," she said in a confident tone. "I'm too nice, too understanding."

She rummaged through her bag and dropped a bulging wad of bills on my desk.

"I mean, what do you expect?" she said, sighing. "I love him."

She got up and slammed the door behind her with a bang that made my skull crack the way dry mud splits in a drought. Nauseated, I threw the tainted bills into my old cast-iron box. Then I grabbed a bottle of mineral water from the fridge and downed half of it. The chill made my eyes tear up. I spent the rest of the day taking care of my piles of paperwork and writing up reports on past assignments. That night, my cell phone started ringing as soon as I arrived at my gate. I didn't answer and instead watched the bats taking flight over my house. I wanted to be forgotten by the world. I wanted to forget myself.

The phone kept ringing, and I was finally forced to see who was calling. It was Kansaye. I picked up, sighing.

"Yes?"

"Have you lost your mind?"

"What?"

"Don't fuck with me, Solo!"

"I don't know what you're talking about," I replied, irritated.

Strangely, Drissa wasn't waiting at his post. I honked the horn. No answer.

"I explicitly told you to walk on eggshells, and you, you couldn't find anything better to do than to stir up shit!" Kansaye blared in my ear.

I honked again.

"Listen, I just told you I don't understand why you're angry. So for fuck's sake, settle down and tell me!"

I was expecting an explosion of cursing. But Kansaye actually seemed to calm down.

"All of Bamako knows about the contract…"

"Jesus Christ, what contract?"

"The one you made with Farah Tebessi to hunt down and eliminate her sister's killers."

"What? That's bullshit!"

"So you're denying it?"

Still no Drissa. This had never happened in the ten years he had worked for me. What if he was hurt?

"I'll call you back as soon as I can."

"No! Don't hang up—"

I ended the call and slipped the cell into my pocket. I got out of my car and called for Drissa but heard only the distant laughter of kids playing on the riverbank. My phone started vibrating furiously. Kansaye was fit to be tied. I glanced around. The street was deserted, except for a scraggly dog rifling through the ruins of an abandoned house. I pushed open the gate. It wasn't locked. Something wasn't right. It wasn't like Drissa to leave the house wide open. I went inside.

10

He was lying on the floor with orange adhesive tape around his ankles and wrists. His mouth was taped shut, and his eyes were moving excitedly, warning me—I realized too late—to watch out for the person behind me. I crouched beside him. A split second later I felt an excruciating pain at the back of my skull. The room rocked, and the floor rushed toward me.

Two seconds, an hour. I couldn't tell how much time had passed.

When I came to, I was on my side. Pain was shooting through my head in rhythm with my heartbeat. For that matter, I hurt all over, and I felt as weak as a newborn. But I wasn't tied up. I didn't know whether that was good or bad. Across from me, Drissa was still in the same position. His coloring was ashy, and he looked terrified.

"It'll be all right, Drissa," I croaked. "Don't worry."

A pair of shiny black dress shoes entered my field of vision. Only someone with OCD could keep his shoes that clean in a country full of red dust.

"Nice shoes," I said. "Italian, right?"

The right heel struck my head. It hurt like hell. Black flies danced before my eyes, and I thought I was going to pass out again.

"Italian leather," I grumbled. "I'm sure of it now."

"Mr. Camara, your attempt at humor is too childish for a situation as serious as this."

I managed to roll on my back. The guy was wearing a linen suit. From my perspective, he seemed huge. He was white and had a square face with the features of a fifty-year-old. He looked bored. I figured he was hoping to carry out an unpleasant but necessary task as quickly as possible. Two men were standing a few feet back. Black guys with the build of boxers. Two monsters beefed up on steroids. No doubt these were the guys who had been following me in the Land Cruiser. The white guy looked at his right shoe, which I had had the temerity to defile with blood and drool. His barely contained anger burned behind his eyes. He bent down, took a tissue out of his pocket, and started cleaning off the affront. His technique was precise.

"You're an unpleasant person, Mr. Camara. A notorious alcoholic and certified shit-stirrer. Everything about you annoys me."

"Where do you get your info—from my fan club?"

"And you feel the need to be witty. But I imagine you're doing that because you're slightly anxious about the predicament you're in."

"In fact, I'm scared as all hell. If I didn't have a sense of decency, I'd be shitting my pants."

"That doesn't surprise me."

The dandy spoke with feigned refinement and a slight accent, which I couldn't put my finger on. He walked over to Drissa and squatted. He studied him with his head tilted,

showing the same interest as an entomologist about to pin
a bug to a corkboard.

"I've heard some unpleasant things about you, Mr.
Camara."

The call from Kansaye, the contract with Farah Tebessi.
It had to be that.

"There is no contract," I said, getting up on my knees.
"That's the hysterical ramblings of a woman who's grieving
over the loss of her sister."

The dandy turned away from Drissa to look me up and
down. His eyes penetrated me like an ultrasound.

"I believe you, Mr. Camara. You see, I represent a group
of powerful individuals who do not like it when people
interfere with their business. You'd have to be certifiable
to cross my clients."

"That is not my case."

"And yet I understand you have a tendency to go over-
board. You do stupid things."

"Yes, but that was before. Now I'm in therapy, and I'm
doing much better."

He almost smiled and stood up, motioning to one of his
bodyguards. The guy started walking toward Drissa. He
was brandishing a machete.

"What are you doing?" I asked, terrified.

The guy cut the tape binding Drissa's hands. He pressed
a knee to his shoulder and pinned the old man's right wrist
to the floor. Drissa moaned and looked at me, his eyes
pleading for help.

"What the fuck are you doing? I told you, I don't pose a
threat to your clients, goddammit!"

I tried to get up, but felt sick to my stomach and way
off-balance. Dandy smiled and gave my chest a light kick.
I tumbled backward.

"I'm just making sure you understand the message, Mr. Camara."

He nodded at the giant, who raised the machete.

"NO!"

I cried out like a possessed person, but the machete made its relentless swipe with enough power to slice through Drissa's wrist like a stalk of grain. A red geyser gushed from the bloody stump. I managed to get up and rush to Drissa. I undid my belt and fashioned a tourniquet. His head bobbing, my old friend was on the cusp of unconsciousness.

"It'll be all right. Hang in there," I said, holding him to my chest. His forehead was glistening with sweat.

As I looked up, I realized I was crying like a child.

Dandy and his gorillas had vanished.

11

The Point G Hospital was on Koulouba, one of the five hills that formed a protective wall of mauve sandstone along the northern side of Bamako. The building, which dated from colonial times, overlooked the entire city. It was a former military hospital that had gotten its name from French topographers. On geological survey maps, each hill was given a different letter of the alphabet.

I had stepped away from the emergency area—jam-packed, as it often was—to smoke a cigarillo. From the patio, I watched nighttime cover the city with a blanket of darkness, making the automobile headlights on the major roads dance. I could hear the hectic city sounds, combined with the plaintive songs of nocturnal birds. To my left was the presidential palace, with its impeccable white walls, a sort of Mount Olympus from which ATT presided over the fate of his people swarming down below. I was smoking a second cigarillo when Kansaye came to join me. His driver, armed with a portable radio, was keeping a respectful distance.

"How is he?" Kansaye asked, lighting a cigarette.

"Still in the OR."

"What did the doctors say?"

I shook my head.

"Not much hope. He's old, and he lost a lot of blood."

"We were able to identify the vehicle that was shadowing you. A rental, paid in cash. We're analyzing photocopies of the driver's license the rental agency had on file."

"It's no use. I'm sure they used a fake."

We continued smoking.

I finally spoke again. "When I was a young cop, my colleagues called me the Black Cat. It had nothing to do with my skin color. They claimed I was bad luck. If some asshole threw a manhole cover from the third floor of a building, for sure it would hit the car I was riding in. You know how superstitious cops are. Some guys wouldn't go on patrol with me."

"That's bullshit."

I scrutinized him through the gray smoke of my dying cigarillo. "I don't think so."

From the corner of my eye, I saw the chief of surgery, Dr. Koumare, coming our way. The look on his face was sober. I knew before he even opened his mouth.

"We did everything we could."

He went on for a few minutes with rote phrases of compassion. After finally saying that this was God's will, and there had been nothing anyone could have done, he left, and Kansaye put a hand on my shoulder.

"That doesn't help, does it?"

"Not really. The toubab in me is too strong to believe in fatalism."

"What are you going to do now?"

"Get even." I crushed my cigarillo with my heel.

"Choose the path of reason, Solo. Don't go off starting a war. You won't win. Let time do its thing, and it'll all work out. You'll see. I sneered and let out a sound like nails on a chalkboard."

"Who says I want things to work out?"

12

I had to admit, my belief in a loving and merciful God had taken a few beatings. Not that I had been in any church or mosque lately. No, definitely not. I was in the uncommon position of being both baptized and circumcised, tugged between Jesus and Mohamed. During my parents' divorce, my faith had become a strategic game piece. They battled over it the same way they fought over who would keep the apartment on the Rue Victor Hugo in Lyon. I attended Mass on occasion to please my mom. Although she wasn't a Jesus freak, she did go to church every Sunday. I couldn't help but notice that her animosity toward my father wasn't exactly Christian. She did everything she could to ruin my dad's life. He, meanwhile, prayed to Allah more than once a day, but he still drank, ate pork, and got laid outside the marital bedroom. I listened to their respective sermons with feigned interest, and I would sometimes remind each of them that they didn't exactly practice what they preached. They would invariably respond by saying there was the text, and then there was the spirit of the text. Understanding that was part of growing up they said. Oh, I did understand.

I solved the problem by concluding that what the related books taught was the ideal to which we should aspire, but if we fell short, it was no big deal. For years, my mother thought I was Catholic, and my father hoped I was Muslim, when, really, I was just an opportunistic believer. If religion served my purposes, I was game. In the end, my modest and multifaceted faith disintegrated at the same time my life was destroyed. It made no sense to be scared of a hypothetical hell in the afterlife. I was already there.

Tonight, though, I was a believer. Not a believer in the Trinity or Allah, but a believer in the divine hand that was trying its mightiest to take everything I loved away from me—my wife, my kid, my job, and now Drissa. I cursed God and his vile plans. I spit Him out with vengeance. Now I would handle things myself. And there would be blood!

I rushed from the hospital to Laïco Hotel. A crowd of businessmen, diplomatic envoys, and wealthy tourists filled the lobby, where French still held its ground over English. I didn't care for the place. It was artificial, like a window display. The marble walls were engraved with ethnic motifs, and the furniture vaguely referenced African art, but the décor as a whole didn't fool anyone. We were in an international temple—a soulless place committed to pleasing outsiders. Everything was arranged so that you'd forget Bamako and its poverty-stricken people of varying colors, the stench of sewers, and the incessant clamor. I could have just as easily been in the lobby of a luxury hotel in Geneva or New York. I was reminded of past trips with my son to Disneyland Paris, which I hated just as much. And while I gave in to making the kid happy, I had that same feeling of being taken for a ride.

After entering through the glass doors and being subjected to security, I bolted toward the reception desk and targeted a suit-and-tie receptionist who appeared to be busy behind his marble counter.

"Mrs. Farah Tebessi," I ordered.

The guy pursed his lips as his fingers fluttered over the keyboard of his computer.

"Yes, she is, in fact, a guest of ours. What can I do for you, sir?"

"Tell her I wish to speak with her."

"What name should I give?" he asked, his eyebrow arched.

"Souleymane Camara."

He punched in the number on his landline, which I tried in vain to see over the counter. He waited a couple of seconds, then spoke into the receiver. "Good evening, Mrs. Tebessi. Mr. Camara is at the reception desk and would like to speak with you."

He listened to her response, then hung up.

"Mrs. Tebessi does not wish to speak with you. It's late. She asks that you come back tomorrow."

No point insisting. I shrugged and gave the receptionist a strained smile. I turned and walked away, and when I was positive he was no longer paying any attention, I made a beeline for the elevators. I chose a button at random and got out on the thirteenth floor—which seemed like a good omen. I headed toward a service phone and picked up the receiver.

"This is room service. I have an order for a Mrs...." I waited a couple of seconds, as if I were consulting something. "Tebessi, Farah Tebessi, but I don't have the room number."

I heard the guy grumbling on the other end of the line. "Room 1024."

I hung up.

I took the service stairs and got out on the tenth floor. Walking down the huge hallway with a plush pink carpet and burgundy wallpaper, I felt like I was in a giant gastrointestinal tract. I stopped in front of Room 1024, unable to think straight, and knocked. I waited several seconds. The door opened a crack. And there was Farah Tebessi in only—from what I could see—a white robe. She had clearly just gotten out of the shower and wasn't wearing any makeup. She glared at me through the dark and twisted tendrils of her wet hair.

"What are you doing here? I told the receptionist I didn't want to see you!"

I butted the door open with my shoulder. Her eyes wide, she stepped back.

"You're insane. I'm calling the police!"

I slapped her with the back of my hand, and she went flying to the other side of the room. She landed flat on her back with her robe open, exposing herself to my enraged eyes. I looked away. She moaned as she got back on her feet, her lip busted open. Then the expression on her face changed from shock to defiance. She planted herself in front of me.

"Congratulations! You're fearless against a defenseless woman."

I smacked her again, and she hit carpet. She tried feverishly to refasten her robe around her lower half as I straddled her and seized the collar. I drew her toward me and brought her face within inches of mine.

"As you can see, I am not happy."

She smiled. This time, it was her nose that was bleeding, and her robe was completely undone. My eyes lost their way for a second—a fraction of a second—and she smiled again, triumphantly. I made a fist and grunted. She closed her eyes and let herself drift backward. Because I was hesitating, she let out a gruff and scornful little laugh.

"Hit me or fuck me. Make up your mind!"

She knew I was hard. Defeated, I let go of her and grunted like a muzzled mastiff.

13

She got up, staggering, and caught hold of the mattress on the unkempt bed. She straightened her robe and wiped the blood off her face with the back of her sleeve. I headed toward the minibar and opened it with the toe of my shoe. I got out a mini bottle of Jack Daniel's, poured the contents into a whisky glass, and took a gulp. It burned my throat and brought tears to my eyes.

"Why?" I asked, gazing into the amber liquid.

She headed toward the bathroom and observed the extent of the damage in the mirror. She winced.

"I'm alone in a country that took my sister, and no one wants to help me," she said coldly. "No one gives a shit about the death of a drug mule."

"Your sister was not a victim. She knew what she was doing. Easy money has a price."

She groaned as she splashed her face.

"Pathetic. First you punch me in the face. Now you pummel me with clichés."

I took a large, bitter gulp.

"Everyone is scared of those guys—you most of all," she continued, patting the wound at the corner of her mouth.

"You should be scared too. You have no idea what they're capable of."

I had lost a prime opportunity to shut her up.

"I got a glimpse of that when I identified Bahia's body inside what's pompously called the city morgue." She looked like she was about to cry. "I...I only saw one way to pressure you into helping me. I spread the rumor that I had hired you to avenge my sister's death. I figured that if I couldn't force you to go after those guys, *they* could force you into it. It looks like it worked."

"Even better than you could have imagined. They beat me up and cut off the hand of an old friend."

She froze and turned toward me.

"I'm truly sorry."

"Not as much as I am."

"How is he? Will he recover?"

"Where he is now, no one recovers."

She continued her repair work, using tools from her makeup bag.

"I didn't want things to go this far."

"You should have thought about that before."

She fell silent and covered her bruise with a thick veil of foundation. When she finished, she studied the results and winced again.

"Looks like that's the best I can do."

I took another sip of my whiskey. She had come out of the bathroom again, and she stood in front of me, her hands on her hips and a serious look on her face.

"When we were little, I had to look after my sister. It was my job as the oldest. I was a shy kid, but she was a firecracker. Nothing stopped her, especially not the words 'you're not allowed.' They had the opposite effect. Whatever it was, she'd do it. And she could run like the wind. I could never catch her after she misbehaved. She never had to explain herself, either. My dad, who worked with asbestos his whole life, had spewed out his lungs, and my mother was holding down two jobs just so we could survive. I was the one who cooked Bahia's meals. I was the one who helped her with her homework and made sure she got to school every day. I raised her. My grief is both a mother's and a sister's."

"You think you're the only person who's ever suffered? You're the only person who's been dealt a dirty hand by God?"

She gave me a look full of scorn.

"Who cares about other people's pain? Only mine matters. I'll do whatever it takes to drown my sadness in blood. Even if it's yours. So if you want peace, kill me now, or get lost, because I'll never give up."

I knew she was telling the truth. She'd do whatever it took, even if it meant provoking the killers so they'd finish the job. I took a final sip of my Jack Daniel's and placed the glass on the bedside table.

"I'll find those guys," I said wearily. "And I'll kill them, not because they're a threat to my life—I don't especially care about that—but because I want to. I want them all to die for what they did to Drissa."

I walked over to the door and opened it. Before I stepped into the hallway, I looked back. She was staring at me with crossed arms.

"And once I've finished with them, I'll come back for you."

14

The next morning, I got up early and made my way to the Point G Hospital. I asked for the morgue and was told to go to the basement. Once there I didn't have to look hard for the room. I relied on my sense of smell and my memory from my years on the police force. At the end of the tiled hallway, I approached a guy in a grayish coat that had probably been white at some point. He was roughly the same age as Drissa. I explained that I was there to claim Mr. Diallo's body. He listened intently while chewing on something and asked me to repeat the last name of the deceased.

"Diallo," I said.

He consulted his register, which listed hundreds of names. Seeing that this could take ages, I added that he had died the night before. The old hospital worker's finger continued down the list of dead people. It would pause at every Diallo, and every time I would tell him that it wasn't the right Diallo. I was looking for a man named Drissa. Finally, he reached the end of the list and tapped triumphantly on the entry "Drissa Diallo, born May 9, 1948, deceased May 8, 2009."

He had died the night before his birthday. I claimed the body, and the guy stood up without asking me what relation I was to the deceased. He didn't ask me to show an ID. He just wanted me to fill out the form. As I strained to carry out the task using an old chewed-up pen, he grabbed a set of keys hanging from a nail on the wall. He glanced at what I had written and nodded.

We headed toward the double doors, and after he unlocked them, we entered the morgue itself. I was used to the smell of death, but nothing like this. I felt like running out. The heat was suffocating, even this early in the day, and the stench was so strong, it seemed palpable. Corpses were everywhere—on rusty examining tables and makeshift stretchers. The back wall of the room was lined with pullout compartments, which must have been crammed with stiff bodies. A thick liquid pooled around the drains.

"The AC's broken, and the freezers haven't worked in ages," the old man offered as an excuse.

I indicated that it wasn't a big deal as I suppressed an urge to hurl. He lifted the sheet covering several bodies and called me over.

"Is this him?" he asked, pointing to a corpse.

It was Drissa. The morgue attendant asked how I planned to proceed with collecting the body. I asked what he meant. He looked at the ceiling and sighed.

"We don't have a hearse anymore. You'll have to find a way to transport him on your own."

He helped me carry Drissa's body to my Toyota. I slid him into the back, wrapped in the sheet that had been used to cover him and his dead compatriots. The material was stiff with dried blood and other bodily substances. I gave the old guy a bill. He thanked me with a nod. In the light of day, he looked a little less like his tenants.

"He was your caretaker?" he asked as we were about to part ways.

"How did you know?"

"That's what you wrote down on the form when you claimed the body."

I nodded. "Yes, he was my caretaker and so much more than that."

The guy gave me an appraising look.

"My nephew happens to be looking for a job."

I shrugged, got in the car, and rolled all the windows down.

~ ~ ~

When I arrived at the Martyrs Bridge I found myself trapped in traffic. I held my head in my hands and groaned. A young traffic cop who seemed to be having no luck at getting the vehicles unsnarled walked up to my car, with his whistle between his lips.

"Everything all right, sir?" he asked, letting the whistle drop from his mouth.

I pointed my thumb at the body in the back.

"I'm taking my father home. He just died. So to answer your question, no, everything's not all right."

The young cop glanced behind me, nodded, and took off toward his moped.

"Follow me!" he shouted. He started up his two-wheeler and began blowing his whistle while kicking the cars to create a third lane of traffic. The other drivers glared at me as I followed.

~ ~ ~

I presented myself at my neighborhood mosque with Drissa's body still lying in my Toyota. After I talked with the imam and made a considerable donation, we agreed to proceed with the ceremony that afternoon. The body was removed from the vehicle. With the purification process under way, I returned home for a quick bite. It looked so empty. Milo joined me in the early afternoon and accompanied me to the mosque.

I was surprised to see that a small crowd had gathered in front of the nearby cemetery. There were owners of the shops where Drissa had bought our groceries, other caretakers on our street who had enjoyed chatting with him, and neighbors for whom he had done odd jobs. They had somehow managed to spread the word. All these people lined up to give me their condolences.

When the body was lowered into the ground, only men were present. The cemetery was on the modest side, a sort of vacant terrain where the wild grass had covered most of the burial sites and created a myriad of little mounds. After the imam had chosen a location, we dug the earth with our bare hands. During the night, an abundant rainfall had made the dirt loose and our job easier. Milo and I placed my friend's body, wrapped in a clean sheet, in the makeshift grave. We covered him with stones—so that stray animals wouldn't dig him up—and earth that we packed down by hand. The imam formed a small pyramid with a few pebbles and asked us to kneel. Heads bowed and knees to the ground, we held hands as the imam prayed for Drissa's soul and for his acceptance into paradise. At least, that's what I assumed, as I didn't understand a word of Arabic. I stayed behind for a long time after everyone else left. My knees and back were aching. I stood up with great effort and felt the Serb's calloused hands on my shoulders.

"May the earth lay gently over you, old friend," I said, taking one last look at the grave.

15

I spent the afternoon moping around. That night, I decided to join Milo at Bla Bla, a restaurant-bar on the Rue Princesse on the other side of the river. We ate marinated pork chops and ordered one drink after another. We raised our glasses to our deceased loved ones, and soon we were honoring the departed we barely knew. I lost count. After dinner, we managed to make it up the stairs to La Terrasse, a cross between a rooftop nightclub and a Lebanese diner. A roomful of expats, rich Malians, and dolled-up whores was packed around the bar. The alcohol was flowing like water while the crowd's raucous laughter went sailing into the humid night. Milo had brought some very pure cocaine, which had become rampant in Bamako. We did a line in the john and then a second. I was feeling better, but I knew it wouldn't last. My grief would ambush me as soon as the coke wore off.

A thunderstorm broke out. Rain pounded the tin roof, while the wind bent the trees all around us. Lightning flashed, and each time it lit up the sky, I made eye contact with a curvy woman sitting across from me. Her short dress was so tight, it seemed to be on the verge of ripping at the seams. The young woman next to her looked bored to tears. The radiant one smiled at me, revealing a perfect set of teeth. I raised my glass in a toast to her enormous breasts, which jiggled every time she moved. Milo had had enough. He stood up and staggered over to the bar to pay our tab. When he came back, he slipped the bag of coke into my pocket.

"You need this more than I do," he said.

I offered to drive him home, but he refused.

"You're as drunk as I am, Solo. I'll take a cab. You should too. Just come back for your car tomorrow."

Milo took a deep breath, spotted the exit, and made his way through the crowd, which opened up miraculously. He looked like Moses parting the Red Sea. Now that the bar stool next to me was free, the woman with big tits made a dash for it. She extended a hand. Her fingers were full of cheap rings.

"Hello, what's your name?" she asked in a high-pitched nasal voice they all use at this hour in the night, the voice that sounded like she'd just inhaled helium. I replied and she gave me what was probably her stage name: Samantha. I couldn't drag my eyes off her cleavage. She asked me to buy her a drink. I signaled the waitress and Samantha ordered a beer. We launched into a meandering conversation. Thanks to the alcohol, we quickly became good friends. She was Guinean, and because I was feigning interest, she proceeded to recount her life story. Her kid was with her parents in Conakry while she earned her living by the sweat of her brow. Her fiancé, who sounded more like a pimp than a bashful lover, had recently dumped her for another girl who was probably younger and more profitable. Basically, it was the classic tale of joy and misery. I checked my watch. It was two thirty. I was drunk. Too drunk.

"How about we have some fun?" I asked Samantha.

She agreed and glanced at her friend, who hadn't moved from her stool.

"Tell her she's welcome to join if she wants."

Samantha went excitedly to ask her friend while I paid the bill. I left a generous tip, and when I turned around, my two beauties of the night were waiting for me—the voluptuous fatty and the thin timid one.

~ ~ ~

In the taxi, I wasn't feeling so hot. My head was spinning like a merry-go-round, and my stomach was roiling. I let Samantha take charge. She gave the driver an address, and he nodded. Evidently, he knew the place. The thin one cozied up and began stroking my cock through my pants. I felt bad about getting hard so quickly. Through the grimy window, I watched as Bamako slipped away. I didn't want to bring these girls back to my place. That would have debased Drissa's memory. Not once during our time together did I ever invite a woman back to the house. We had an unspoken understanding. The house was just as much his as it was mine. The bitterness swelled in me as I thought about Drissa. To put him out of my mind, I reached for Samantha's velvety thigh. She smiled at me through a lock of synthetic hair that had fallen over her face.

The taxi parked in front of a Chinese hotel in the Hippodrome neighborhood. These establishments had been multiplying for some time. They had the reputation of being places of real debauchery. The Chinese laborers who worked on all of the city's construction sites came here to dump their wages between the thighs of local whores or girls smuggled in from their home country.

In no condition to negotiate, I paid an exorbitant amount for the fare. I made my way, propped up by a girl under each arm, to the entrance, which was illuminated by a red lamp with decorative writing. Several young Malians on mopeds—also Chinese—were chatting in front of the doors. It was obvious: Mali was in the throes of becoming an offshoot of the Middle Kingdom. We passed them, and one of the guys made a remark behind our backs, which I didn't understand. It set off a thunderous round of laughter. Samantha turned around and gave them the finger. I couldn't say exactly how, but we ended up in a large shadowy room. An acrid stench of morning sweat hung in the thick air. A cruddy bar was in the back. A few guys leaning against it were watching an old soccer match on a wall-mounted TV. Some other men were playing mahjong. They all looked up when we walked in.

"Hi, gang," I said. My mouth felt thick.

They looked away and resumed their respective activities. Samantha asked me for money to pay for a room. I gave her a ten-thousand-franc bill.

"Book the fanciest suite in this picturesque establishment!" I said emphatically.

The skinny girl cackled like a hyena. After taking care of the formalities and buying a few beers, Samantha led us into a dark hallway lit by bare crimson lightbulbs. We passed a succession of plywood doors through which I could hear the sounds of abused box springs, feigned gasping, and deafening moans of ecstasy. Samantha pushed open one of the doors and flicked on the lights. We walked into a room furnished crudely with a bed, graying sheets, and patched mosquito netting. The girls started disrobing, and the smell of their cheap perfume filled the air. Apparently they had no time to lose. I walked with steadier steps to the adjoining bathroom. The corners of the shower were streaked with black mold, and some darkish muck was seeping into the drain. A cockroach scurried across the toilet seat. Tough luck. My drunkenness was going to shit.

"Just pull down hard on the flusher when you're finished," I told the bug.

I walked back into the room, and Samantha started slinking toward me. She wasn't wearing anything except a small chain around her large hips and another around her ankle. Her heavy breasts flopped with each step.

"Is something wrong," she asked me nicely. "You don't like the room?"

I grasped one of her quivering tits.

"It's perfect," I said, smiling.

After paying them, I took out the baggy of coke and drew three lines on a chipped mirror left by God knows what John who had been there before me. We snorted the powder, and the girls undressed me in no time at all. The skinny one—who went by the name of Cindy—folded my clothes neatly while Samantha vigorously washed my cock with fresh water from the cruddy sink. The bug had the courtesy to leave, and my dick was now throbbing inside Samantha's somewhat rough hand. Once the sanitation business was taken care of, we maneuvered to the bed with our uncapped bottles of beer. I lit a cigarillo while Cindy and Samantha, lying on their bellies, took turns sucking me off, taking sips of beer in between.

A hopped-up blow job, I thought as I watched a couple of geckos run across the cracked ceiling. I stuck my dying cigarillo butt inside the neck of my beer bottle. It made a little crackling noise as it drowned in the backwash. The girls put a condom on me and offered the usual compliments about the size of the allegedly coveted object.

And so I fucked them both. I finished with Samantha in doggy position. Her magnificent ass reached toward me while Cindy massaged my balls. The world was capsizing, and I was hanging on desperately to those wide hips while my latex-garnished dick appeared intermittently in the perfect circumference of her cheeks. I was fascinated with a trickle of sweat gliding down her spine. It formed a little damp pool in the small of her back. She moaned with pleasure. It was a lie, but a white lie. I knew it, and she knew that I knew it. I finally came, releasing a squirt as hot as lava. I imagined my jizz was black and sticky like oil. Then came Samantha's big number, the grand finale. She screamed with pleasure, her face turned toward me, her mouth agape, and her wig in disarray.

In situations like this, it's all a matter of protocol.

16

The sun was already high up in the sky when I awoke at my place with my sweaty sheets sticking to my skin and my tongue glued to the roof of my mouth. I got up like an old man and stumbled toward the kitchen. I stretched with difficulty. My back cracked like old floorboards. I prepared a strong espresso, and with my cup in hand, I went to the patio and sat down in one of the wicker chairs facing the river. The somber ripples on the water mirrored my mood. I savored my caffeine, keeping my ears open for the slightest noise. But there were no familiar sounds. No cooking noises in the kitchen, no happy whistling in the garden. Cars were piling up on Martyrs Bridge. I picked up my phone and called Kansaye.

"Hello, Commissioner," I said when he answered.

"Good morning, *Warakalan*."

"I decided not to follow the path of reason."

Silence on the other end.

"I need to know if I can count on your help." I picked up a cigarillo and lit it while I waited for a response.

"What do you want?"

"The phone records of Bahia Tebessi's last conversations."

I held my breath.

"Go see Pierre Diawara. He'll tell you what he's got. I'll make sure he does it."

He ended the call.

I got up with a grunt and headed toward the bathroom. After a quick shower, I shaved. My hand was shaky, but I managed to avoid cutting myself. I put on some clean clothes and wrapped my tagelmust around my neck. To finish up, I examined my reflection in the mirror. Aside from my bloodshot eyes and ashy complexion, I looked almost human.

I went to the garage and got out the small pickax that Drissa used for gardening. Armed, I headed for the traveler's palm growing next to the house. Behind the tree, I started digging. The tool quickly hit metal. I continued digging by hand, fished out a large steel box equipped with a combination padlock, and swept away the coat of sticky dirt. I placed the box on the ground and leaned against the house. A huge bird, a kind of blue magpie with a long tail, came down next to me and started hopping around in the grass. I sighed and bent forward to get a closer look, but the bird chirped and flew off. I turned my attention back to the box and dialed the numbers 0-7-10. Alexander's birthday. Inside a plastic bag was a small black briefcase. I opened it.

There it was, held captive in a foam cushion.

I ran my fingers over the cold steel of the barrel and shivered.

I spent part of the morning oiling and cleaning my weapon. After checking to make sure it was in functioning condition, I loaded the two magazines with 9mm cartridges. It felt strange to be going through this once-familiar routine again. I threaded a clip inside the grip, brought the breech back with a swift tug, testing a cartridge, and slid the Glock in the small of my back behind my belt.

I was ready for the rest of the day. I hailed a taxi, fetched my SUV, and an hour later presented myself to a disheveled-looking guard at the police criminal investigations unit, commonly called the BIJ for *brigade d'investigations judiciaires*. Mali was once the French Sudan, and even though it has been an independent nation for a half century, vestiges of French rule still remain. For example, Mali loved its technocracy and overly complicated acronyms that stood for simple concepts. The guard, who appeared to be doubling as a secretary, informed me that Chief Diawara was expecting me, but he was busy at the moment. I went in without knocking, interrupting an old man who was blabbering about something. Pierre was politely listening with half-shut eyes. His face brightened when he saw me, and he cut short the old man's speech, taking him by the elbow and escorting him to the door while offering reassurance that he would come through for him. After closing the door behind him, Pierre Diawara slumped into his chair.

"The old man was pleading a case for his grandson, who's charged with armed robbery. Despite statements from the victims and the fact that some of the stolen goods were found in the kid's home, the man insists on trying to convince me that he wasn't involved."

"Meanwhile, you're forced to entertain him."

Pierre smiled and looked at his watch. I did the same. Eleven thirty. He reached into one of his desk drawers and opened the small fridge behind him. Then he poured us tall glasses of bourbon mixed with a little soda.

"It's tradition. What can I say..."

We clinked our glasses and drank in silence. Pierre was from a Christian family. This had hurt his career, because the best positions always went to Muslims. His pals from the police academy had been promoted ages ago, but he remained on the sidelines. He didn't harbor any resentment, though. For Pierre, the glass was unfailingly half full.

"Kansaye asked me to give you the details on the Tebessi case. But to be honest, we don't have much."

The media frenzy had certainly died down, and the case would soon be of no interest to anyone. Farah was right. No one cared about an insignificant drug mule. Still, I was a bit skeptical about Pierre's claim.

"I imagine you've investigated Bahia's phone," I said, placing my glass on his desk.

Pierre took out a sheaf of documents bearing the Orange Mali phone company logo and handed it over to me.

"You can have these," he said. "They're photocopies."

I took the papers, put on my reading glasses, and quickly scanned them. They were, indeed, the young woman's cell phone records.

"Can you identify this one?" I asked, pointing to the last number Bahia Tebessi had called.

The listing indicated 5:38 p.m. Tuesday. The conversation had lasted two and a half minutes.

"No problem." Pierre scribbled the number on a piece of paper.

There was a knock at the door. A young guy about twenty years old stuck his head in.

"Hello, Grandfather. I've brought what I owe you."

In Mali, calling someone grandfather regardless of familial relationship was a sign of respect.

Pierre waved the young man into his office. The latter gave me a nod and took out a wad of crumpled bills.

"Here you are."

Pierre took the money without counting it and slipped it into one of his pockets.

"Solo, this is Yacouba, one of my drivers."

I knew that Pierre had a fleet of a dozen taxis that he rented out weekly. Thanks to the money he earned from the cabs, he didn't have to engage in any shady activities to feed his family. In Mali, a police chief could not live on his salary alone. It was worse for lower-ranking cops.

I shook the driver's hand.

"Tell me, Yacouba, would you be interested in earning a little money?"

It was like asking a blind man if he wanted to see.

The driver nodded enthusiastically.

"You bet, sir. Who couldn't use some extra cash?"

"I'd like you to put me in contact with the taxi driver who picked up the young French woman from the narcotics unit."

"The girl who was murdered?"

I nodded.

He shook his head. "That could be complicated and also—"

"Don't worry. No one will know you're working for me," I said as I pulled out a ten-thousand-franc bill from my wallet.

I handed him the money, which he took after a pause of several seconds.

"Two more like this one if you find the guy. It was last Tuesday, late afternoon."

Yacouba nodded. "I'll call you as soon as I get any information," he said.

We exchanged phone numbers. The taxi driver said good-bye to Pierre and left.

17

Intent on finding a burner, I ended my meeting with Pierre. I quickly spotted a shop, which was little more than a shanty: loose boards and rusty sheet metal. Inside I found exactly what I was looking for: Chinese phones—poor imitations of designer brands. I purchased a cell and a chip for a ridiculously low sum and headed for the French Cultural Center on Independence Avenue. It was an ocher-colored building surrounded by a thick wall and topped with a multicolored tiara of bougainvillea vines with sharp thorns. At the entrance, officers from the mobile security group were killing time in their plastic chairs. In the past few weeks, all of Bamako had been buzzing with rumors of an attack. Al-Qaeda in the Islamic Maghreb was constantly threatening French interests, which were considered an obstacle to the Salafi movement in West Africa. A suicide bomber had just blown himself up in front of a French Cultural Center in Mauritania.

I went through security without any trouble. Everyone knew me here. I had chosen the center for what I wanted to do because I doubted that anyone would try to kill me so close to half a dozen armed officers, albeit sluggish ones. I sat down at one of the tables in the central court that served as a café and ordered a coffee. Several young Westerners and Africans in dreadlocks were sitting nearby, drinking sodas and beers. They were talking loudly and cracking jokes. Most were wearing T-shirts inspired by Che and Bob Marley, exhibiting them like a brand names, more for status than real interest.

I lit a cigarillo, took out the cell, and slipped the SIM card into its compartment. I pressed the "on" button—written in English—and, to my huge relief, the phone lit up with its welcome message. There was just enough battery power for what I had to do. I took out the last page from the phone records and dialed the number Bahia had called the day she was killed. Someone picked up on the fourth ring.

"Yes?"

It was an African man's voice. I was sure of it. He sounded hesitant, or maybe worried.

"We have to talk," I said in an authoritative voice.

There was a long silence. Then: "Who are you and what do you want to talk about?"

I took a drag of my cigarillo.

"Bahia Tebessi and her murder."

Silence again.

I'd have to bluff. "I know who you are and where you live. If you don't want me telling the police and the press what I know, I'd advise you meet me right now at the French Cultural Center."

"You're crazy! I don't know anything about—"

"You'll recognize me easily. I'm mixed race. I'm wearing a white linen shirt, brown khaki pants, and a blue chèche."

I hung up.

18

I was on my third coffee when a guy who looked like a condemned man on his way to the gallows walked in. He was a slender African with black skin and the aquiline features of someone from the North, probably a Songhai. He quickly scoped out the room, pausing on me. Once he realized that I was staring at him, he stepped back, as if he were going to leave. I stood up and waved him over. He looked surprised.

"Me?" he asked.

That was the voice I had heard on the phone half an hour earlier.

"Have a seat," I said in an unequivocal tone.

The man hesitated and then complied, pulling out the metal chair across from me. It made a loud scraping noise, causing everyone to turn around. He gave them an apologetic look and sat down. There was a thin layer of sweat on his forehead.

"What the fuck do you want?"

The people around us had resumed their conversations.

I gave him a kind smile and punched him in the solar plexus. The jab was quick and undetectable to anyone not paying attention. The guy's eyes widened with surprise and filled with tears. He opened his mouth like a fish thrown onto the barge, but no sound came out. His diaphragm was blocked. He gasped for air.

"Don't worry," I said. "It's uncomfortable, but you'll be back to normal in a few seconds."

I glanced around us. No one seemed to be noticing my pal's distress. I took advantage of the fact that he was preoccupied to search his pockets. I quickly found a wallet from which I pulled out a Malian driver's license. On it was the name Sinaly Maïga. Sinaly: the guy who had welcomed Bahia at the airport and served as chaperon during her trip.

"Nice to meet you, Sinaly. My name is Souleymane, but you can call me Solo."

"You're crazy," he said between coughing fits.

"Without a doubt. Talk to me about Farah Tebessi."

"I don't know—"

"Tsk, tsk… You're about to say something you'll regret."

He looked like he was about to get up. "I'm going to tell the police that you assaulted me."

"All right, let's do that. Let's go straight to police headquarters and talk about Bahia Tebessi's murder. I forgot to mention that you're implicated in a drug-trafficking ring."

"That's bullshit. You can't prove anything. Did she give you my last name?"

I remained silent while he celebrated.

"I knew it! Do you realize how many Sinalys there are in this city?"

"The investigators will really be interested in the conversations you had with Bahia. You were one of the last people she spoke to."

"You can't do anything to me. You don't know who's behind all of this. You've got no idea."

His voice was getting louder, and people were turning around to stare.

"Calm down and use your brain—if you've got one," I said. "Who's going to take the blame? You think your friends will show you unswerving loyalty? I don't. I think they've got the perfect fall guy. You're the one who'll be taking the hit for everyone else. And they'll have no trouble finding your replacement while you're rotting away in Bamako's big house."

He didn't say anything for a few seconds. "They can't do that," he finally responded. "I know things. If I talk—"

"If you snitch to the police, you won't be around for long. You'll end up in the river ripped open, like poor Bahia. No, it's better that you don't go to the cops. As for me, I won't say shit. This stays between us, like a confessional. Lips are sealed, mum's the word, all that jazz."

He looked at me, wringing his hands.

"Yes, I'm the one who picked her up at the airport. I slipped her the money—"

"I know all that," I interrupted. "Just tell me who had her killed and why."

"I have no idea. I'm a nobody. Me and some other guys fly coke into France. It goes to the projects around Paris. Penny-ante stuff. If you want my opinion, the people who did this are some kingpins."

"Why would these guys want to kill an ordinary mule?"

"No idea. They don't show me the big picture. All I do is take care of the girls and give them the stash before they board the plane."

He looked tormented. Even if I hounded him for hours, I wouldn't get anything else out of him. I'd have to tackle the problem from another angle."

"Okay, then tell me about the day she got out of jail. She called you. What did she want?"

"She wanted me to pick her up, but I didn't want to. It would've put me on the cops' radar. So I suggested that she call her boyfriend."

"Her boyfriend?"

He nodded. "While she was at the Hotel Olympe, I introduced her to a friend of mine. They hit it off."

"So why didn't she call him first?"

"When he found out that she was involved in a drug deal, he stopped taking her calls. He didn't want any complications in his life. But I wasn't the one fucking her, so it was on him to do what had to be done."

"What had to be done?"

"Don't get any ideas. I mean pick her up from the police station. He's a good guy. He's not into the drug scene. He doesn't have to be. He's got a sweet job…"

"Where can I find him?"

19

The sun was beating down on the tarmac of the Bamako-Senou International Airport, and the windsocks were drooping woefully in the burning air. I could feel the sweat dripping down my back, pinning my clothes to my skin. The simple act of breathing was painful.

"Stéphane Humbert?"

Wearing brown overalls, he was working on the engine of a small propeller plane. He turned to me with an inquisitive look on his face and gave me an affable smile.

"Yes?"

We were just outside the second-to-last hangar in the section of the airport where the smaller airlines were located. Through the half-open metal doors, I could see another plane. It was a bit bigger, a twin-engine. On the back wall a sign bore the logo of a line of heavy-construction equipment. Just below it was the name of a corporation: Cartagena Export, Mining and Trading.

Humbert placed a socket wrench on a large toolbox, picked up a rag, and wiped his hands and face.

"Who are you?"

"Souleymane Camara," I replied, holding out my hand.

He shook it. His grip was firm. The man was in his thirties, I figured. He had an athletic build, and his green eyes, which flashed with a mischievous flame, probably worked well on the ladies.

A bastard.

"What do you want, Mr. Camara?"

"Call me Solo. I'm investigating the death of Bahia Tebessi."

His face froze.

"You're a cop?"

"No, a private detective," I said, handing him my card. "I've been hired by her family."

He measured me up, not saying a word, and then looked at the card.

"Let's get out of this furnace before we get heatstroke," he finally said.

He led the way around the hangar. Behind the building, a few woven chairs and a cooler perched under a big mango tree appeared to be waiting for us.

"Wait here a sec. I'm gonna go wash off my hands."

When he returned, Humbert pulled two chilled beers out of the cooler. He removed their caps and handed me one. We clinked our bottles and took long swigs.

"What exactly would you like to know?"

"I'm being paid to find out who's responsible for her death."

Gazing into the distance, he digested the information.

"Mr. Camara... Solo, I have a good job, an honest job, and I'm married to a wonderful, well-educated Malian woman. She went to college in France and has given me three beautiful kids. I love my life here in Bamako. I wouldn't want to lose it all over a silly, childish fling."

"So you don't deny that you knew her?"

He smiled ever so slightly.

"Why would I? You're here. That means you know."

"Stéphane, I'm not here to ruin your life. I just need information."

"Ask your questions."

"How did you know Bahia?"

"A mutual friend introduced me."

"Yes, Sinaly."

Humbert studied me. I figured he had the right to know his pal was a little shit.

"So he was the one who gave you my name?"

I nodded.

"We met at Star Night, a club on the Rue de la Princesse."

I indicated I was familiar with the club.

"My wife and kids were visiting my parents in France. I had too much to drink that night, and she... She was amazing. Eventually, we wound up naked in her room at the Olympe."

He paused. "I can't believe she's—"

"Did you see her after that?" It wasn't really a question.

"Several times. I even took her up in my plane."

"Yeah? Where'd you fly?"

He hesitated. "We flew west to the Kayes gold mine region, near Sadiola. I needed to drop off some equipment for my company."

"Which company?"

"Cartagena. It's a Spanish mining corporation that extracts and sells gold. I do runs between the mines and Bamako. Since it's a beautiful region, I figured I'd kill two birds with one stone. We picnicked and made love in the great outdoors."

I offered him a cigarillo, but he declined. I lit one for myself. In the distance, over the Monts Mandingue, steely clouds were building up. They'd soon be dumping rain on

Bamako. I exhaled a dark ring, which dissipated in the air—my modest contribution to the approaching storm.

"She called you the night she was released."

He turned white and looked at his shoes.

"How did you know that?"

"What happened, Stéphane?"

"My wife had just come back from France. Bahia couldn't have called at a worse time. I told her I couldn't help her, that I was at work. Afterward, I called a cabbie I know to go get her. It's all I could do."

I sneered at him. "How generous of you."

He looked hurt and lowered his head again.

"It was the only solution I could think of that would keep my family out of it and keep me from feeling like a piece of shit."

"Did it work?"

"No."

I got up and sighed.

"One last question. Were you in contact with her again after that call?"

"No. She tried several times to call me, but I turned off my phone. I learned what happened in the paper."

20

On my way home, the sky grew darker. More than a typical storm was brewing. This was the kind of squall that had the power to clear streets. The temperature took a nosedive, and a whoosh of air shook my car. I leaned forward, peering at the clouds and trying to determine whether I'd make it home before the sky unleashed its wrath. I got my answer in no time. Scathing gusts of wind began to rip apart the tin roofs of miserable shacks packed with the poorest residents of Bamako. Metal scraps and plastic bags soared through the lightning-laced sky like birds of ill omen. A dense rain beat down, bombarding my Toyota, studding the ground with small geysers and filling the gutters with muddy water. I had to put on my brights. It looked like nighttime in the middle of the afternoon. All motorcyclists had stopped under the bridges. Suddenly, I was blinded by a set of ultra-powerful headlights in my rearview. I blinked, cursed, and readjusted the mirror. When I turned around, I saw a large black SUV on my tail, just inches from my bumper.

It was the same vehicle that had followed me before.

They were back.

It was about time.

Clever tricks wouldn't get me out of it this time. Anyhow, I didn't want out. I got off the main route at the first intersection, committing myself to the suburbs of Bamako. Driving over the rain-ravaged dirt roads, I passed the deserted Kalaban-Coura market, with that damned SUV still goosing my tailpipe. I was in a state of feverish exhilaration, wavering between yellow-bellied fear and white-hot anger. I thought about Drissa, and hatred welled up in me. A hatred so pure, so ample, so perfect, I felt like a suicide bomber putting on his explosives vest. I pulled out my Glock, turned around, and tried to aim despite the jolting of my car as it sped over the ruts. Finally, I made an educated guess and fired through the rear window of my poor Toyota.

The crack of the bullet made my ears ring. The glass shattered in intricate crystals and landed all over the backseat. The black 4x4's windshield looked star-spangled. I pulled the trigger two more times.

Whistling was all I could hear in my right ear. Behind me, the vehicle swerved and crashed into a brick wall, which collapsed on it. The engine howled like a wounded animal. Shrieking victoriously, I slammed on the brakes, and my car skidded to a stop. I opened the door and jumped out. I had something of an out-of-body experience as I looked at the scene. In no time at all, the street had become a muddy torrent. Water was up to my ankles, and gusts of wind whipped my face. How had my old Toyota made it this far? I didn't have time to mull it over. I slogged over to the SUV. With my still-fuming Glock in hand, I opened the driver's-side door. The man was vomiting blood. One of my bullets had hit his throat. The other guy had hit the windshield. His head was bobbing, but he was still lucid, and he was struggling to open the glove box.

I rushed to the other side of the car. When I put my hand on the handle, he shoved the door open and sent me flying. I wound up on my back in a deep puddle. I dropped my Glock and swallowed a huge mouthful of thick mud. I sat up and spit the stuff out. I was still trying to catch my breath when an enormous figure appeared in front of me. He leaned in close, his face dripping blood. The passenger and the guy with the machete were one and the same. I desperately grappled for my weapon. But before I could find it, the monster grabbed me by the neck and threw back his other arm. I saw his coconut-sized fist coming toward me and lowered my head. The cranium is the hardest bone in the human body and those in the hand are the weakest. Still, it was an incredibly rough blow. My brain bounced in my skull like a pinball machine. The guy howled and released me, leaving me to fall flat on my belly. He straightened up, holding his hand. For sure, it was fractured.

I kicked and flailed in the thick muck, and then my hand grazed something hard—the butt of my Glock. Re-armed, I was hoping to turn things around, but the muscleman had grabbed me by the ankles and was dragging me along. I swallowed more mud. Half-choking, I managed to turn on my back. A remarkable kick to the side sent me flying. I landed in the puddle again, groaning and on the verge of losing consciousness. The man was now straddling me, holding a huge rock in his good hand with the obvious intention of smashing my skull. Luckily, I hadn't let go of my weapon. I fired twice. The first bullet went soaring into the wilderness. The second struck his knee. He wailed and staggered as he tried to balance himself, still holding the menacing rock.

"Motherfucker!" I yelled.

I aimed and shot at his elbow. Bull's-eye. The rock fell right between my legs. I strained to get up and look him in the face. The giant, who was gushing blood every which way, emitted a strange flutelike cry. Yelling, I thrust myself on him, grabbing his neck as my knee dug into his gut. He tumbled like an uprooted tree and pulled me down with him. I emerged from the water coughing and spitting up. Now my opponent was vomiting out his insides. I crawled over to him and planted myself on his chest. As I sat on him, he lifted his head toward me, his eyes pleading and tearful.

"His name was Drissa," I rasped.

The giant looked confused.

"The guy whose hand you chopped off."

A faint glimmer flashed in his eyes, and he smiled. "The old guy," he said.

With my hands around his neck, I pushed his fat head under the muddy water and held it there. He thrashed, but with little energy. He had lost a lot of blood. He puked again as I brought him back up.

"His name was Drissa, and he was my only friend," I said.

"Drissa," he repeated, nodding weakly.

He was trembling like a child, but I didn't give a shit. In my head, I was watching the machete swoop down, the dark blood burst from Drissa's raw stump, and the terror rush into his eyes.

"Who was that toubab who was with you that day?"

"He's my boss."

"I know he's your boss. I want his name."

"Rafael."

"Rafael what?"

"Rafael, that's it."

I could read in his eyes that this was all he knew. No surprise there. Strongmen like him could be picked up in dozens of Bamako weight rooms. For a little money, they'd kill anybody, no questions asked. I wouldn't get anything else out of the guy. I dunked his head under water, and as he thrashed listlessly, I whistled a nursery rhyme that Marion used to sing to Alexander when he had a hard time falling asleep. I could feel the water rushing into his lungs like a wineskin filling up.

My car had agreed to start after wheezing, sputtering, and spitting out a plume of black smoke. Soaked and shivering, I was finally driving on a paved road. On the passenger seat, I had thrown a business card found in the glove compartment of my followers' SUV. I had to search their vehicle quickly, as I feared the police would show up at any moment. The card, which had been lying under the unused black revolver, bore the logo of Cartagena Export Mining and Trading—the company Stéphane Humbert worked for. On the back was a scribbled cell phone number. I was trying to think, but my mind was in a spastic state, and I realized I was muttering a string of incoherent thoughts like a crazy person. I tried to pull it together. Eventually I started to calm down. What I needed to do now was go home, warm up, and figure things out. Atop the Monts Mandingue, sunlight was peeking through the shreds of gray clouds.

21

As I neared my house, I saw a young man sitting outside my gate. When he spotted my Toyota limping along the road, he dashed to open the gate and let me pass. I parked in the bougainvillea-covered driveway while the kid closed it again. With a wide smile, he hurried to greet me.

"Hey, boss!"

He gave me a worried look.

"Are you all right? Did you get into an accident?"

I looked at my soaked and torn clothes and touched the painful bump on my forehead. I shrugged and turned my attention back to the kid. He was twenty at the most. He was wearing a filthy pair of jeans and a ripped T-shirt. But over his shoulder he was sporting a stylish gym bag— the kind that was popular with kids in Europe and the United States.

"Who are you?"

"My name's Modibo Touré. My uncle suggested that I come to see you."

"Who's your uncle?"

"He's in charge of the morgue at Point G Hospital."

"Ah!"

We were standing on a thick bed of bougainvillea pet-
als. The storm had ripped the flowers off the vines.

"I remember him," I said after a long pause. "But that
doesn't explain what you're doing here."

"Well..." he replied, rubbing his chin. "He told me you
were looking for a caretaker."

"I don't need anyone. Get out of here."

The young man shifted his weight from one foot to the
other. "I can cook too."

"Scram," I told him.

The kid lowered his head and turned to walk away.
I shouldn't have taken my anger out on him, but I had
just lost Drissa. I knew it wasn't the kid's fault. In Africa,
one man's death is a living man's opportunity. The gate
creaked, and he was about to leave.

"Hey, Modibo!"

The boy froze and turned around.

"Can you read and write?"

"Yes, boss," he said proudly, "I love books and—"

"Get the broom and sweep the driveway, please," I said
in a weary voice.

He flashed an enormous smile.

I went inside to take a piping-hot shower while Modibo
swept with great delight. When I finished, my cell started
vibrating on the living room bureau. Still drying my hair,
I checked the screen.

Hamidou Kansaye.

I couldn't possibly guess what the police commissioner
wanted from me. I hesitated, then picked up.

"Tell me it wasn't you."

"It wasn't me."

He sighed.

"There are two bodies at Kalaban Koura. A couple of
musclemen who were done up real bad."

"What makes you think it was me?"

"I don't know—the style. Plus some witnesses saw a vehicle at the scene that sounded a lot like yours. So please don't bullshit me."

I threw down the towel and lit a cigarillo.

"It was me," I said, exhaling a cloud of smoke.

There was a long silence at the other end.

"I would have liked the bullshit better."

"You need to make up your mind."

"What the hell am I going to do with you?"

"Stick me in jail, I guess."

"Why'd you kill 'em?"

"I was driving along, minding my own business, and these guys got right on my ass. I've never been a fan of tailgaters."

"Don't fucking mess with me!"

"Those were the guys who chopped off Drissa's hand."

Kansaye was speechless for several seconds.

"So it's over then? You got 'em?"

"Those men were only tools. They were no more important than the machete that sliced Drissa's wrist. I want the decision men, the ones who killed Bahia Tebessi. I'm going to clean house and stop at nothing, unless you decide to arrest me."

After a long silence I realized that Kansaye had ended the call. I shrugged and put the cell back on the bureau.

22

No police cars outside my house. No cops ringing at my door. Kansaye was turning a blind eye for the moment. I was safe for now, but I knew one day or another he'd slap a charge on me. I had thrown on a pair of khaki pants and a clean shirt. Modibo had finished his sweeping and—after rummaging through Drissa's tools—was trimming the hedge with a pair of rusty clippers. He was putting a lot of energy into his task, as evidenced by the sweat glistening on his forehead. I called for him. He came rushing over, wiping his face on his already cruddy T-shirt.

"You'll be staying in Drissa's room. It's got electricity and AC. There're some clothes in the dresser that should fit you. Have at 'em."

"Does that mean I'm hired?"

I cooled his excitement. "Consider it a trial period."

We negotiated his salary, and I ended up shelling out more than I should have. I always sucked at money-related stuff. Modibo was ecstatic. He thanked me over and over.

"All right, all right," I muttered. "Just do the job right."

I went to my office, turned on my computer, and started doing a little Internet research. Cartagena had come up several times and that was certainly no coincidence.

I needed to take a closer look at them. According to the company's site, Cartagena had a branch in the ACI-2000 district of Bamako. The company claimed to be involved in real estate, mining, and contracting not only in Mali, but also in the rest of West Africa. A Ukrainian by the name of Mike Kedzia was in charge of regional operations. I couldn't find much on the guy, aside from a few articles on some African websites praising his generosity. In one photo he was handing over a check to a Bamako artists association. He appeared to be in his midthirties. He had jet-black hair and a heavy face. I engraved his image on my brain before shutting down the computer. I rewarded myself with a beer and offered one to the kid, who had begun tidying my things in the living room.

He politely declined. "No thank you, boss. It's haram."

"What a drag," I said to myself, sighing.

He left the living room and reappeared a few minutes later with an armful of dirty clothes.

"What are you doing?" I asked with some irritation.

"I'm going to wash your clothes. They're very dirty."

"Not that tagelmust, kid."

"But it's full of blood and dirt."

"Not the tagelmust," I said, grabbing the piece of old cloth and tying it around my neck.

By nightfall I was ready to go. I gave Modibo a few instructions, which he jotted down with a chewed-up pen in a little notebook. I grabbed my digital camera with a medium telephoto lens and got in my car. This time the engine had no problem starting. I drove onto the dirt road. In the rearview, Modibo was giving me a huge good-bye wave beneath the streetlamp. I couldn't help but smile. With one hand on the wheel, I entered Milo's number in my cell phone. The Serb picked up after the third ring.

"Yeah."

"Always friendly."

"What do you want, Camara?"

"Your help. They tried to kill me earlier today."

Silence. I narrowly dodged a suicidal moped rider as he cut in front of me.

"I'll send you a pal of mine," Milo eventually replied. "His name's Rony. He's a dependable guy. Lebanese."

"Is he expensive?"

"Less than a one-way ticket to hell."

"When is he available? This can't wait."

"I'll call him now."

He hung up. I reached the paved road and forced my way into the traffic, which was packed with *soutrama* vans and spluttering mopeds. I crossed the Pont du Roi Fahd and, once on the other side of the river, headed toward ACI-2000. I didn't have to search long. The building was just behind the US Embassy. It was a small three-story building surrounded by a cinder-block wall. Above the entrance, a sign announced Cartagena Inc. Just to the side, three security guards were chatting and drinking tea. A bit farther away, the minarets of the big mosque were standing tall in the stifling night.

I parked and turned off my headlights but kept the engine running because I didn't want to lose the AC. I settled into the seat, but it wasn't long before the mosquitoes invaded my personal space. I really did have to get that back window fixed. As I tried to fend off the nasty creatures, I saw several people leave the building. Based on their appearance, I guessed they were office workers, secretaries, and accountants.

Just as I was losing hope, a white guy emerged from the front entrance. He was wearing dark slacks and a short-sleeved pastel-colored shirt. He was talking on his phone. Judging by his wild hand gestures, I figured he was arguing.

A shiny new Mitsubishi Pajero pulled up, and the guy, still shouting, hopped in the back. Despite the distance, I recognized him. It was the Ukrainian—Mike Kedzia. The car took off. I gave the Pajero a good lead before setting out to follow it. The drive lasted only a few minutes. We had traveled a little over a mile when the vehicle stopped in front of a big villa. The driver honked, and the gate opened. It was operated by a caretaker in a brown security uniform. I slowly passed the house, discreetly peering into the courtyard. I glimpsed Kedzia getting out of the car with the phone still glued to his ear. The caretaker closed the gate.

I made a U-turn a bit farther away and parked in a dark area, with the camera propped in my lap. From where I was, I could see the comings and goings, but nothing else, as the high walls blocked most of the villa. The mosquitoes quickly smelled blood and started attacking. I wondered if I'd be in for another bout of malaria. The time passed, The bites multiplied. Then a huge Hummer pulled to the front of Kedzia's house. Two men got out, and through my camera lens, I recognized the driver. It was the dandy. I didn't know the second guy, who appeared to be a fair-skinned Hispanic in his fifties. He had the build of a sumo wrestler. I took several photos of the two men and the Hummer's license plate. The men rang the bell, and the caretaker quickly let them in. I checked my camera screen. The pictures weren't perfect, but I could make out the features of the man who was responsible for Drissa's death.

"Nice to see you again, Rafael," I muttered.

23

Hours went by, and despite my attempts to stay awake, I nodded off several times. The bump on my head was throbbing and all I wanted to do was take a shower and dive into my fresh sheets. I checked my watch—1:48. I yawned so wide, my jaw cracked, causing my head to throb. Finally, I decided to go home. I had enough information, and I didn't want to risk being discovered by staying any longer. I carefully started the car and drove with the lights off until I made it to the paved road. Only then did I turn on my headlights. When I arrived home, Modibo was catnapping in a camping chair in front of the gate. Half-asleep, he got up and let me in. After closing the gate again he walked over to my car.

"Your friend is here, boss."

"My friend?"

"Yes, you know, your Lebanese friend."

He pointed to a tall figure who was smoking in the yard.

"You let him in, just like that?"

"He told me he was working for you," Modibo answered. "Was I wrong to do that?"

I gave him a wave of the hand to indicate it didn't matter and joined the guy by the pool. He was well over six feet tall and had to weigh more than two fifty. Most of his bulk looked like muscle. He was sporting a thin Errol Flynn-style mustache and a hideous Hawaiian button-down shirt. I could see the butt of a large caliber semiautomatic sticking out of his pants.

"You must be Rony," I said.

He nodded and threw his finished cig in the grass, which Drissa had just cut. A giant bat grazed the surface of the pool. It hardly made a ripple on the oily water.

"How long can you stay?"

"As long as it takes," he said.

His voice was gravelly, most likely because of the Gauloises he seemed to favor. He pulled a pack from his breast pocket and lit another one. With the fresh smoke hanging from the corner of his mouth, he held the pack out to me. I declined.

"I'll explain the situation—"

He held up his hand, indicating he didn't need to know.

"You're a friend of Milo's, and I'm here to protect you. If someone attacks you, I'll kill him. That's all there is to know."

"As for money—"

"Work that out with the Serb. He's my agent, so to speak."

We stood there silently, watching the bats perform their ballet in the sky.

~ ~ ~

The next day, I awoke at dawn. My whole body ached. I dragged myself to the shower, and the water did me good. In the bathroom cabinet, I found some codeine pills that were only a year past their expiration. I swallowed two. If I didn't know better, I would have sworn that the guy looking back at me in the mirror was on his last legs: bloodshot eyes with dark circles, ashy skin color, and deep purple bruises.

I turned away, aware that the bruises would fade and I'd look better eventually, but I'd always have one foot in the grave and the other on the edge. I didn't have a deep desire to live, but I didn't have the balls to die either.

I dispelled my morbid musings and got dressed. The aromas of coffee and toast greeted me as I walked into the living room. Rony, cigarette in hand, was seated at the table, watching CNN on low volume. Modibo was filling his cup. The kid's face lit up when he saw me.

"Good morning, boss. Would you like some coffee?"

I grunted, which he took as a "yes." I watched Modibo as he served me. He was so good-hearted and enthusiastic. It was nauseating. The phone rang before I could dwell on my unkind thoughts. I picked up and immediately recognized the distinguished voice with the hint of an accent.

"Mr. Camara?"

"Yes."

"Do you recognize me?"

"Yes, and it won't be long before I discover exactly who you are. It's only a matter of days, hours maybe."

"I was thinking we might be able to reach a compromise, an honorable way to resolve this misunderstanding, which isn't doing our affairs any good."

"For me, there's only one honorable way out of this, and that's breaking your neck."

I ended the call. Rony turned toward me.

"That was them?"

I nodded.

"All right, our options are clear now. We kill them."

"Or they kill us," I contemplated.

I examined my cup and eventually brought it to my lips. I was skeptical, as I had downed too many cups of Drissa's dreadful coffee.

"Something wrong?" Modibo asked, the anxiety evident in his voice. "It's no good?"

Shocked, I shook my head.

"No, it's very good. No worries."

It hurt me to think that this kid's coffee was better than Drissa's. It was excellent, actually. Once again, he grinned from ear to ear, and for some odd reason, it made me think of music. Young people, it seemed, lived to the beat of lively African rhythms. But when old people opened their mouths, only sharp notes came out.

"Don't stand there like an idiot," I told him. "Your work won't get done by itself."

He nodded and brought me some toast in a small basket. I was carefully buttering it when Rony abandoned the TV to send me a cheeky smile.

"What?" I grumbled.

~ ~ ~

I was about to close my car door when I felt resistance. Rony was holding it open, refusing to let go.

"Don't take this one."

"Why not?"

"They know it now. And plus, this car's worn out. I sent for another one. It's parked on the street."

We walked down the path, and sure enough, a huge SUV topped with a roof rack was in front of the house.

It was an older Land Cruiser J80, but not as old as my Toyota, and it was clearly in mint condition. Rony handed me the key.

"It's got a turbocharged HD engine. I think you'll like it."

I opened the door, slid behind the wheel, and inserted the key. The Land Cruiser started without any of the sputtering I was used to. The engine roared when I revved it and settled into a healthy purr when I let up. I smiled at Rony.

"Yeah, I like it."

The Lebanese man walked around the vehicle, opened the passenger-side door, and slid in next to me.

"What are you doing?"

"My job."

"I didn't ask you to come. Just stay here and watch the house."

He turned toward me and gave me a stony look. "Just so it's clear between us, I'm not asking your permission. I'm doing my job. If someone kills you, I'll have to explain it to the Serb, and that's not something I want to do."

I searched for a good comeback, but nothing came to mind. I settled for a pathetic one. "You could at least take the wheel for me."

"I'm your bodyguard, not your driver."

I grumbled as I pulled away from the house.

24

I parked in front of the Department of Mines, Energy, and Water in the river neighborhood. Rony got out of the car before I could say anything. I was beginning to regret having asked the Serb for help. In the department's inner courtyard, drivers were napping under mango trees beside a line of shiny SUVs that even a senior official or local minister couldn't afford on just his government salary. I sought directions from a security officer, who pointed me toward the mining claims sector. I went up a flight of stairs, with my Lebanese bodyguard still on my heels. I knocked on an office door. Rony lit a Gauloise and leaned against the guardrail. I shook my head, then entered. I was now in the secretary's office. She looked like a real boss-lady type in her sixties and wearing a lavish boubou. She assessed me from behind the thick lenses of her tortoise-shell glasses.

"How can I help you?" she asked.

"I'd like to consult a mining file."

"And what gives you the right to do that?" she responded.

I decided to get on my high horse. "My right as a citizen of Mali to have access to such documents."

"Are you a reporter?" she asked. Her haughty look had disappeared. She was biting her lip.

I gave her a wink. "If I were, I couldn't tell you."

She was silent for a few seconds before handing me a grimy piece of paper.

"You'll have to fill this out."

Unable to find a flat surface to write on, I sat down on the other side of her desk and pushed her things out of the way to fill out the form. The secretary sighed but didn't say anything. I completed the questionnaire and handed it back to the woman, who read over it quickly.

"Did I get them all right?" I asked, pretending to be concerned.

"This'll do," she said. Her scornful look had returned. "We'll call you back once you've received authorization."

"You see, I'd prefer to receive that authorization today."

"I'm telling you to leave now," the woman said, rising from her chair. "We'll call you."

I settled into my own chair and put my feet on her desk, shoving her clock aside in the process.

"No point in putting you to the trouble. I can stay here and wait, seeing as I have nothing special to do today—or tomorrow, for that matter."

Clearly insulted by my shoes on her desk, the secretary started muttering vague threats. With my request in hand, she headed toward a door at the back of the room and opened it. From where I was sitting, I couldn't hear what she was saying, but I assumed she wasn't giving me a very flattering introduction. After a few words were exchanged she reappeared and motioned for me to enter. I found myself in a second office. A man in traditional garb stood up. His desk was covered with piles of what were obviously pending files.

"My secretary says you're making a fuss."

"I certainly was not. I was merely trying to meet with you, as you're the one who makes the decisions."

He gave me a bothered look. He was tapping my consultation request form in front of him.

"Mr. Camara, you shouldn't do what you're doing."

"What's that?"

"You shouldn't be acting rude and confrontational."

I pretended to reflect on his comment.

"Ah, I get it! The Malian government already has a monopoly on this type of behavior."

He smiled.

"It's a monopoly enjoyed by every government in the world. Why would it be any different for Mali?"

"I hadn't seen things in that light. As for my request..."

The government employee took the paper I had filled out and slid it under a huge and wobbly pile of similar requests.

"It'll be processed in due time."

We stayed there, staring at each other with fake smiles plastered on our faces. I asked him how his family was doing. He explained how hard it was for a good Muslim to take a second wife. Should everyone live together, or should each of the wives have her own home? Then there were the expenses. The two wives had to be treated the same, after all. And then there were the children. They all had to be provided for.

As I nodded in agreement, I opened my wallet and slipped three ten-thousand-franc bills onto his desk. The man pretended to ignore them, calling in his secretary and giving her several instructions. The woman disappeared, but not before I had the chance to give her one of my irresistible winks. The department head feigned diving back into his paperwork. The bills had disappeared. After several minutes of silence, the door opened again, and the secretary reappeared with a meaty file. I noticed her nails were painted purple as she dropped the file in my lap. A small cloud of red dust rose up on impact. I coughed and swatted the air in front of my face. She gave me a cocky smile, and I turned back to the bureaucrat.

"Can I take this home to read?"

"I'm afraid not," he said without looking up from his papers.

I unwound the string that held down the flap of the manila envelope and began reading.

A good hour later, I left the mining claims office. Rony was waiting for me with the ubiquitous Gauloise hanging from his mouth.

"Did you get what you needed?"

I lit a cigarillo. The acrid fumes made my eyes water.

"So it seems."

25

On the drive to the Niarela district with Rony, I suggested that we stop for a pizza. He responded with a shrug. I parked the Land Cruiser in front of Chez Milo and waved to the crippled man, who was walking toward us with his crutch, ready for duty.

"You got a new ride, boss?" he asked as he ran his hand over the hood.

"Yeah, you like it?"

"Very much, I'll take good care of it."

We fist bumped. Inside the restaurant, Milo was at a table, a pince-nez held together with tape perched on his nose. He was working the buttons of a noisy old calculator. The Serb was doing his accounts, and judging by his furrowed brow and clenched jaw, I figured he wasn't enjoying it. He looked up when Rony and I walked over to join him.

"What do you boys say to some drinks?"

A waiter came over. He jotted down the three-beer order in his notepad as if he were afraid of forgetting it. He returned a few moments later with the beers. The three of us took hearty swigs, and when we put our glasses down there was foam on Rony's Errol Flynn mustache.

"So, how's it going?" Milo asked. "He's not busting your balls too hard?"

"No, no," I said generously while shaking my head. "But to be completely honest, Rony is a little clingy, and I was wondering—"

"I wasn't talking to you, Camara," the Serb interrupted.

Rony nodded to indicate that everything was going all right, and I was ashamed of the speech I had prepared in the car to get rid of my burdensome Lebanese watchdog.

The waiter brought over the pizzas. As always, it was a four seasons for me.

Milo watched me while I got to work on the crunchy thin crust. The African sun had etched razor-thin wrinkles under his blue eyes. They gave him a kind of quizzical look.

"What about you? How's your investigation?"

I claimed that I didn't want to involve any of my friends—especially him—in my ugly affair, but the Serb wouldn't hear of it.

"We're past that point. I'm already involved—because we're friends. Now spit it out."

Deep down, I was relieved by his insistence. It made me feel less alone. And so I told him about Cartagena, the Spanish company that handled real estate and did some consulting but made most of its money mining gold in Kenieba, which was in the Kayes region, near the Senegalese border. According to the government file, this revenue was enough to turn heads, more than three hundred million dollars the previous year.

Milo whistled. "Three hundred million? Fuck, these guys aren't nobodies. What are you thinking, Camara?"

"Well, long story short, I started getting followed once Farah Tebessi spread the word that I was investigating her sister Bahia's murder."

"A run-of-the-mill coke-smuggling case," Milo said. "There's one in the papers every week."

"Nevertheless, the information I collected all leads to Cartagena."

The Serb shook his head. "I don't see a company with through-the-roof revenues getting involved in transporting a few kilos of coke," he said.

"You're right. It doesn't make much sense."

"What if the girl was killed for some reason other than drugs?" the usually silent Rony asked.

"It's a possibility, but I'd be surprised if that was the case," I answered.

I continued my story, but Rony's question was nagging at me.

"The file that I checked out at the Department of Mines, Energy, and Water had another interesting detail," I said. "Next to Mike Kedzia's name was Rafael Ortega de la Torre. He's C-level."

"C-level?"

"That's senior management, company executives, chiefs." It was the second time Rony had spoken up.

The Serb looked at him in surprise. "How'd you know that?"

"I served with the Army Rangers. Don't you remember?"

"Oh shit, I forgot you're half Yankee!"

"Getting back to the senior managers," I said, annoyed.

"Don't get your panties in a twist, Camara. So who is this godfather?"

I maintained the suspense by staying quiet a few seconds longer. Then I leaned toward the two men. "I'm almost positive that he's the dandy who had Drissa's hand chopped off," I said. "The guy I plan to have a little chat with one day soon."

"We could just take him out now. Save us some time," Milo suggested eagerly.

"That would be a bit premature," I said, straightening up. "Especially since I'd like to figure out what's going on here. We'll take care of him once I have everything I need."

The Serb and the Lebanese man nodded in agreement. We finished our beers and pizzas in silence.

26

After lunch, Rony asked me to drop him off at his brother Paul's place. Paul managed an inn called the Abeille in the Hippodrome neighborhood.

"I have to deal with some family business. Don't do anything that'll put you in danger while I'm gone."

I assured him I'd be careful and said I'd be back at four to pick him up. I sighed in relief as I started the car again.

Alone at last.

When I asked Milo for help, I thought he'd send a security guard to watch over the house, not a nanny who'd tag along with me twenty-four-seven. I arrived in ACI-2000 and parked near the Cartagena building. I walked around to the back and was pleased to find the Pajero parked beneath a canopy of palm tree leaves. Nearby, the driver was chatting with some security guards. I went up to them and introduced myself as a driver for some rich toubab who had a meeting at Cartagena's offices. The guards were friendly guys. They invited me to join them and made space on their wobbly bench under an ancient tree. I had a seat across from Mike Kedzia's driver, who was sprawled in a camping chair. They offered me some tea, and we started talking. I made the most of the situation by complaining about my hellish boss—the toubab forced me to work overtime without pay.

"He goes out to chase gazelles at the bars every night, and I have to wait in the car while he enjoys his little hookups."

The guards and the driver shook their heads in sympathy.

"No, seriously, it's not right," Kedzia's driver said. "He could easily take a taxi. We have families, don't we?"

"It's true. I never see my wife and kids anymore. I'm sure it's the same for you."

The driver, who introduced himself as Coulibaly, shook his head. "Thank God, my boss doesn't go out much."

"He never goes to the bars?"

"Rarely. Only when he's meeting his colleagues."

"Is he French?" I asked innocently.

"No, I think he's Russian or something like that."

"Although with his Russian colleagues, he must drink a lot."

Coulibaly sipped his syrupy tea.

"I know his colleagues are Spanish. Whenever they talk business, it's in Spanish. He doesn't want me listening."

I pushed further.

"I thought Russians loved to party. The vodka, the girls..."

Coulibaly looked at us with a knowing expression and added in a softer voice, "In the two years I've worked for him, I've never seen him with a woman. But sometimes he invites young men over—only black men. They usually leave well after midnight."

One of the guards shrieked. "That's forbidden! It's haram. No, that's not right at all."

We all nodded.

I checked my watch and started to get up. I told my new friends that my boss had to be somewhere, and if I didn't hurry, he'd be late. I returned to my Land Cruiser and made myself comfortable, tuning in to Radio France International. The hours passed. At five thirty, Coulibaly—behind the wheel of the Pajero—pulled up to the building's main entrance. Mike Kedzia slid into the backseat. I noticed he was wearing a lightweight business suit, instead of the casual attire I had seen him in the first time.

"So, ya got a date, Mike?" I murmured as I pulled out.

I followed the Ukrainian man's car, relying on everything I had learned during my years as a criminal investigator to stay right with him in Bamako's messy traffic. After a good half hour, we crossed through the Dar Salam neighborhood, and Kedzia's car appeared to be headed in the direction of Gabriel Touré Hospital. The car stopped on a residential street just behind the hospital, at a large house surrounded by a high wall loaded with surveillance cameras. We weren't alone. Dozens of official and company cars were parked chaotically along the street. I drove by Mike Kedzia, who had been dropped off at the front entrance. I parked a bit farther away. Before getting out of the car, I slid my Glock under my seat.

A French flag was hanging limply from a pole in the motionless air. This was the French ambassador's private residence. I was tempted to turn around, but managed to convince myself there'd be no harm in having a look. I approached the large half-open front door. Two French police officers with handheld metal detectors were checking for invitations. I joined the line, glad I had made the call to ditch my gun. In front of me, a large Malian man in Western clothes was talking in Bambara to a woman in traditional garb. I spotted a thin piece of cardboard sticking out of the man's pocket. After taking a look around, I carefully swiped the card. When it was the guy's turn to approach the officers, he reached toward his pocket to pull out the invitation. Unable to find it, he apologized and started going through his other pockets in search of the damned card. As he searched, I stepped in front of him and presented my invitation to one of the cops. He glanced at it, then quickly ran the metal detector over me and waved me in. I entered the ambassador's gardens as confused and thunderous declarations rose up behind me. The guy was swearing to God he had had his invitation on him only a few seconds earlier.

27

Expatriates, officials in uniform, and wealthy Malians were exchanging pleasantries in the gardens of the ambassador's residence. Waiters dressed in white were carrying trays underneath the foliage of ancient trees. A doe wandered among the guests, begging to be petted and fed. Holding my glass of Champagne, I happily joined the crowd. Mike Kedzia was talking to some guy whose beard, round shape, and wrinkled face fit the bill of an old foreign affairs politician. My phone vibrated in my pocket. Rony. This was the third time my Lebanese helper had tried to reach me. I didn't pick up.

"What the hell are you doing here, Solo?"

Someone grabbed my elbow. Turning around, I found Kansaye. He was glaring at me.

"Commissioner, how good it is to see you here," I said, feigning pleasant surprise.

"You've gone completely insane. How could you show up here, on French territory, where you're a wanted man," he said through clenched teeth.

"Hey, I've got my invitation, so be nice, please. And anyway, why are you here?"

In a large group of expatriates, I noticed a man in the white uniform of the overseas gendarmes, who were in charge of security at the French embassy. And he was throwing glances in our direction.

"Stop clowning around, Solo. That guy who's watching us—he's the attaché to the French embassy's security and a police inspector who might know you from the days when you were the talk of the town back in your other homeland."

"Never met him. What is this little shindig anyway?" I asked to change the subject.

"It's a party organized by the ambassador to encourage cultural patronage in Mali."

"Really? I never knew you were a fan of the arts."

"You are such a pain. I was invited by my friend, the security attaché."

The man in question was now approaching us with glass in hand. He was tall and thin and directing his curious eyes at me. Kansaye started walking toward him, leaving me behind. The two of them greeted each other warmly, and then the French cop made it clear that he wasn't going to be diverted.

"So, Hamidou, why don't you introduce me to your friend?"

For the first time ever, I saw the police commissioner lose a bit of his impeccable composure.

"Sure… This is Souleymane Diabaté. He's the son of an old friend of mine."

"Diabaté, you say? That means you're a griot?"

In Mali the Soumano, Kouyaté, and Diabaté families were traditionally griots—poets and musicians who passed on the countries oral heritage. I let out a loud laugh. "So I see you're familiar with our cultural history, sir. Let me assure you, there've been no traveling musicians or story-tellers in our family for a long time."

The cop stared at me with resolve.

"Is there a reason you're looking at me like that?" I asked, beginning to squirm inside.

"I'm sorry, but I almost mistook you for a piece-of-shit lowlife I know of: a fellow Frenchmen named Camara. The resemblance is striking."

I faked a shiver. "Phew. You had me worried for a second there. And what did this person do to get on your bad side?"

"He's a traitor. He was a police officer until he turned—"

I could sense Kansaye tensing up beside me. "How about we refresh our drinks..." He hailed a waiter.

"To finish answering your question, Mr. Diabaté, he killed a lot of people," the officer continued. "But the worst part is that he killed one of our own men, and then he fled the country. Like most French cops, I've been familiar with his most-wanted poster for years. And it's got a great photo. We only recently learned that he had sought refuge in Mali. It's his father's homeland."

I couldn't help challenging him in his little game.

"*Was.*"

"Excuse me?"

"It *was* his father's native country. Souleymane Camara's father died four years ago."

"So you know him?" the officer asked, furrowing his eyebrows.

"Bamako is really a village, and this man you're de-scribing as a killer in your country is hailed as a hero here. Everyone knows who he is."

"Yes, I've heard that. The White Leopard and all that crap."

"It's not bullshit," Kansaye chimed in. "As a private detective, Camara has solved some important cases. And he doesn't make his poor clients pay."

The security attaché dismissed Kansaye with a sarcastic laugh.

"It's because he's got a lot to make up for."

"I believe that," I said calmly. "But might it be possible that he's not quite as bad as the scumbag you describe?"

"You give him far too much credit," the police officer thundered. "A hundred cases solved free of charge couldn't make up for what he's done."

People were turning around and staring at us.

"And what would you do if you found yourself face-to-face with him?" I asked in a final attempt to provoke him.

A waiter filled our Champagne glasses. I emptied mine like a parched horse at the trough.

"I imagine I'd spit my hatred in his face and arrest him," the officer said. "After all, we're on French territory here."

I smiled confidently as Kansaye stepped in.

"Come now, Christophe. You know that's just nonsense. If you arrested Camara—who, by the way, has Malian citizenship—we'd all get wrapped up in an endless roll of legal and bureaucratic red tape. Mali, just like France, does not extradite its citizens."

The security attaché took several moments to reflect.

"Now that I've gotten a better look at you, I don't think the resemblance is that strong," he said coolly.

He walked away and rejoined the group he had been with.

"Looks like he's not a big fan of yours," the police commissioner said.

"He has his reasons," I replied, giving Kansaye a friendly pat on the shoulder. I ditched my chaperone and headed toward the Ukrainian.

28

Mike Kedzia was at the bar, waiting for a glass of Champagne. I carefully positioned myself in his way, so that when he turned around he couldn't avoid bumping into me. Some of his drink splashed on my shirt.

"Oh, I'm so sorry," he said. "How clumsy of me."

I assured him no damage had been done. "There's hardly anything on my shirt. You know what they say about Champagne not staining."

"Either way, please accept my apologies."

"It's nothing. But your glass is practically empty now. Allow me to fix that."

I took his glass and handed it to the bartender. At the entrance to the mansion, the ambassador—a tall, fiftyish, and undeniably distinguished man with white hair—had begun his speech, and the partygoers were edging closer to hear him better. Darkness had spread throughout the gardens. In this part of the world, the night nudges out the day as abruptly as someone flicking off a switch. Swarms of insects were swirling around the glow of the outdoor lanterns.

I extended my glass toward Mike Kedzia, who was staring at me.

"Souleymane Diabaté," I said as an introduction.

"Mike Kedzia."

We clinked our glasses.

"To unlikely encounters, which are always the best kind."

"Yes, to excellent encounters."

The fact that he didn't recognize me boded well. I wondered how much he knew about Rafael's bloody dealings. And I couldn't help noting that Kedzia didn't correspond with my mental image of a pitiless drug trafficker.

We chatted for a half an hour or so and I seized the opportunity to question my new friend about his professional activities. He dished out the same spiel that was on the company website. He asked me what I did for a living, and I told him I was a visual artist, even though I didn't know exactly what that entailed. When pressed for an explanation, I went off on a tangent, which seemed to satisfy him. Judging by the ravenous looks he was giving me, I could have just as easily been talking about how poorly the CFA franc was doing.

"I'm not a big fan of small talk," I ended up saying. "And I'm hungry for more than bite-size appetizers."

Kedzia looked at me even more intently. "You're not afraid people will notice our absence?"

I chuckled. "Are you kidding? These people are too busy showing off to care about what anyone else is doing. Plus, I couldn't care less about what they'll say."

The gendarmes saluted us as we left. Once on the street, Kedzia took out his cell phone.

"Who are you calling?" I asked.

"My driver. It'll only take a few minutes for him to get here."

"No need to bother him. Where do you want to go?"

"My place, if that's all right with you."

Deep down, I let out a sigh of relief.

"Not at all. That's perfect. My car's parked nearby."

We walked to the Land Cruiser in silence. As I inserted the key I asked which way—to keep up appearances. He directed me the whole way, and I was thankful that his hand didn't stray to my thigh. I parked on the street and stealthily retrieved my Glock from under the seat after he got out. His caretaker opened the door and greeted Kedzia while making it a point to ignore me.

"Perhaps you should send your staff home," I whispered. "I can be very loud when I get excited."

Kedzia gulped and nodded enthusiastically. The Pajero was parked under an awning. I looked around nervously. This would be a bad time to bump into Coulibaly, but luck seemed to be on my side. The house was decorated tastefully. Kedzia pointed to the bar and asked me to pour us some Scotch while he told his staff to go home. He left like the wind. It almost made me feel bad. When he returned, a bit out of breath and all excited, he accepted the Scotch and took a big swallow. He coughed, and his eyes filled with tears.

"So, are we alone now?" I asked.

"The house is all ours until tomorrow morning."

He came close to me and swept his hand over my chest. His fingers stopped on the buttons of my shirt. Just as he started to undo one, I grabbed his hand. Using a technique I learned in my anti-gang training, I bent it backward—hard, but not hard enough to break it. He cried out in pain and then grunted when I shoved him away with a kick in the gut. He fell into an armchair. I pulled out my gun, and his face quivered at the sight of the black barrel.

"No, please don't kill me. I have money—"

"Shut your mouth."

"I'll give you whatever you want."

"Just shut up."

He quieted down at last, and his eyes filled with tears. Still pointing my gun at him, I checked the windows to make sure we were alone. Reassured, I closed the heavy drapes.

"What do you want from me?" he said after a few moments.

"Answers to my questions," I responded, sitting down on the couch across from him.

"What questions? I don't understand. I'm just a simple—"

"Don't bother," I said wearily. "Let's be clear. I'll ask the questions, and if I think you're lying, I'll put a bullet in your knee."

He nodded and stared at me with terrified eyes that were so wide, I thought for a minute I might have a hard time killing him.

"Let's begin. Why did you have Bahia Tebessi killed?"

"Who?"

I leaped up and struck him with the barrel of my weapon.

"Don't hit me," he wailed. "I don't know who you're talking about!"

The Glock's sight had left a bloody groove on Kedzia's face. He sobbed as he reached up to touch it.

"My face… You've disfigured me."

I sat down again. I could already feel a migraine coming on. Doing this was very unpleasant.

"Consider yourself lucky. You can still walk. I promised a bullet in the knee, and I won't be so nice the next time. So?"

Kedzia sobbed again.

"I… I don't know anything. I'm not the one who gets things done at my company."

"What company?" I asked, already knowing the answer.

"Cartagena. I take care of ordinary operations and accounts. I'm an accountant by training. For everything else, it's my associates who—"

"What associates?"

"Rafael and Rodrigo."

"Why do they want to take me out?"

His eyes got big again. He looked at me as though I were the devil himself.

"My God, you're Solo Camara?"

"In the flesh," I said.

"They want to eliminate you because you're interfering with their plans, and your timing couldn't be worse," Kedzia said, wringing his hands.

"How's that? What are you and your pals up to?"

He lowered his voice. "It's a huge operation. If we mess up, our directors in Spain won't forgive us. Rafael doesn't want to take any risks."

"You should shut your huge trap, Alejandro."

The voice cracked behind me like a horsewhip. I spun around. Rafael Ortega de la Torre was pointing an enormous shiny revolver at me. He wasn't alone. Two henchmen, also armed, were just behind him. One was the fat Hispanic guy I had already seen with him. I assumed he was Rodrigo. The other was black, of the same ilk as the two guys I offed.

"Set your gun down, Mr. Camara."

I hesitated.

"Now!" he barked.

Defeated, I put down the Glock.

"Now slide it toward me."

I kicked the weapon toward the Spanish man. He picked it up, keeping the outsized revolver pointed at my belly.

"You really like the glitz and glam, don't you, Ortega? Big shiny guns and all that. You know what they say about guys with big weapons?"

"They generally don't say anything unless they're looking for a bullet."

I let out a little laugh, but I shut my trap when I saw his jawline tighten. Then Rafael put his revolver in his shoulder holster and raised my Glock. He started walking toward Kedzia.

"Good thing you got here in time. He was going to—"

Rafael fired twice. Kedzia collapsed in his chair, his eyes bulging.

"You're fired, Alejandro," Rafael said, sneering at Kedzia. My gun was smoking in Rafael's hand.

"What the fuck, Rafael," Rodrigo shouted. "You know who that fag is."

"I couldn't take the fairy anymore," the Spaniard replied calmly. "He was going to fuck everything up anyway."

"Christ, Rafael," Rodrigo groaned. "We're dead if the Colombians hear about this."

"Fuck the Colombians."

Rafael approached me, still holding my Glock. He put his free hand on my shoulder.

"You're subject to bursts of violence, Mr. Camara, aren't you? So it won't surprise anyone when the police discover that you killed a poor businessman who tried to get in your pants."

"That's a bit far-fetched, don't you think?" I countered.

"This is Mali, Mr. Camara. It was your weapon that killed him, and I'm sure you were seen together at the French ambassador's house. That's basically all it'll take to make you the killer. If, however, someone starts asking the wrong questions, I just have to shell out a few million to fix the problem."

"How did you know?" I asked.

"His driver. He recognized you when he saw you arriving with his boss, and thinking Kedzia was in danger, he called us. So there you have it."

Rafael gave Rodrigo a little nod, and before I could say anything else, the back of my head exploded. I was in an ink-dark well with a million sparkling shards of something whirling around me.

29

I felt wild ponies galloping in my head. Trying not to vomit, I opened my eyes. Total darkness. From the bumping, I could tell we were in some kind of vehicle. The space was so cramped, I was folded up on myself. They had thrown me into the back of a vehicle—with someone else. The other person was leaning against me. He let out a little muffled cry.

"Mike? Hold on there, man. I'll get us out of here."

I got no response. I was drenched in a hot, sticky substance draining from his body. I twisted in an attempt to find a latch to open the rear door, but my hands were tied behind me—with what I assumed was a zip tie. I had used them all the time when I was a cop. The plastic was digging into my wrists, and I was unable to free myself or even reach my cell phone, which was in my pocket. I fought anyway, groaning in powerless rage.

I tried to ignore the Ukrainian, who was agonizing next to me. I should have felt relief at the prospect of bringing my shitty life to a close. Loneliness had been eating away at my soul for so long. Unfortunately, that wasn't the case. I no longer wanted to die. Not like this, at the hands of that piece of trash Rafael. I wanted to live and choose my own death.

"Motherfucker!" I roared, rupturing my vocal chords and eardrums.

I heard laughter from the front seats.

And now I could feel it building inside me—the fury. It swelled, and when it peaked, an even stronger wave followed. I surrendered. I had no more fear, no more pain. I was a raging mass. Drissa, my wife, my kid, and all the other victims who littered my life. These sons of bitches were going to pay. They were going to pay for even the deaths they knew nothing about.

The vehicle stopped. I heard doors slam and footsteps come my way. Someone opened the back. I saw the prominent silhouettes of Rodrigo and the Malian backlit by streetlights.

"All right, come on," Rodrigo said. "The sooner we do this, the sooner we can call it a night."

The Malian nodded. He started pulling me out of the back like a sack of cement. I pounced on the chance to send a solid kick to his chest. He stumbled backward and wound up on his ass, his eyes bulging from his skull. I had put every ounce of my rage and frustration into that blow. With legs like springs, I leaped out and rammed Rodrigo. I knocked him over too, and we rolled on the ground. My opponent tried desperately to find his weapon as I stayed with his massive body. With my hands still tied, I sought his throat with my teeth. I bit as hard as hell and tore off a piece of flesh, or rather fat, which ran uneasily down my throat—I almost chucked it back up. Rodrigo wailed like a pig and struck me in the face with the butt of his automatic, which he had finally found. My cheekbone and the top of my eye socket were smashed, but that only fueled my hatred. I pursued one of his ears, which I sank my teeth into with a roar. I crunched the cartilage and chewed the lobe as he tried to push me off. I could feel a warm dampness on his pants and realized he had pissed himself. Unfortunately, someone was tearing me away from my feast. I spit out a piece of flesh and growled like a wild animal. Now I was getting pummeled so hard, I thought I would pass out again. I ended up flat on my stomach, my blood running into the dirt, making a sticky mud. Close by, I could hear Rodrigo whining like a child.

"Get up."

It was Rafael's voice. I didn't move, and I heard the characteristic sound of a gun being cocked.

"Have it your way, Camara. We'll just have to drag your body inside. That's all."

I managed to get on my feet. My head was ringing, and blood was spouting from my face. Rafael was standing in front of me, holding my Glock and staring at me as though I were some rabid beast. He looked disgusted—but also fascinated.

"You're a real whacko," he said. I picked up a tinge of admiration in his voice.

Aided by the Malian, who had regained his breath and his energy, Rodrigo straightened up. Blood was gushing from the side of his face where there had once been an ear. He was also missing a good chunk of meat from his throat. I had come damned close to killing him.

He aimed his gun at me.

"I'm going to fucking kill this son of a bitch. Get out of the way, Rafael."

"Not outside, dammit!" Rafael thundered.

"What the fuck! Do you see what he did to me?"

"Shut up! You should've been more careful."

I glanced around. We were in a dirt courtyard outside a large decrepit building. Nearby, there were warehouses and other buildings that looked like factories. This was Sotuba, Bamako's industrial neighborhood. My Land Cruiser was parked in the courtyard and the back was still open—it was the vehicle my captors had used to drive the Ukranian and me here. The Malian pulled Mike out and threw him over his shoulder. With satisfaction, I saw that he was giving me wide berth.

"Fuck!" Rodrigo moaned. "I need to see a doctor. Human bites are the worst. I could get an infection." Had I been in a better mood I would have told him that I was the one more likely to get sick from the chunks of him that I had eaten.

Rafael sighed and pushed me toward the building. Inside, the huge space, tiled from wall to ceiling, was empty, with the exception of a few workmen's benches and abandoned tools. Rails with hooks ran along the ceiling.

It was an old slaughterhouse.

The Malian dropped Mike on one of the tables used to butcher meat. He was still alive. His chest was moving in sync with his erratic breathing. Rafael handed my Glock to Rodrigo.

"If he moves, put a bullet in his leg," he said as he fixed his eyes on me. "I want him to see what happens next."

"You can count on me, *Jefe*."

Rafael rummaged under a bench and pulled out a mask and an apron covered with brownish splatterings. I closed my eyes when I understood what he was planning. He put everything on and walked over to some shelves where there was an old chainsaw—the kind used to take apart the carcasses of slaughtered animals. I realized I would have been better off letting the Spanish guy do away with me in the courtyard.

30

Rafael gave the cord a tug, and the bitch of a motor started right up, without even a sputter.

"Impressive, no?" the Spanish man bragged as he revved his power tool. "Runs like clockwork. I love this thing."

He walked toward Kedzia, the chainsaw purring like a cat awaiting its pâté.

"He's still alive, Ortega," I cried out. "At least finish him off first."

"That's exactly what makes this so exciting, Camara—him being alive. Haven't you seen *Scarface*?"

"How sick are you, Ortega?"

He wasn't listening. He set up shop on the right side of Kedzia's inanimate body, raised the chainsaw, and slowly brought it down on his victim's shoulder. With an ecstatic smile on his face, he began cutting. The machine sliced flesh and bone. Garnet-red geysers shot toward the ceiling. Kedzia's body shook with convulsions so violent, I thought he might fall off the table. Then the Spanish man sliced off his head, and Mike's body was still. Now he was a simple chunk of meat.

Blood was everywhere. I felt like throwing up and had to look away. I wasn't the only one. The Malian and

Rodrigo were also looking elsewhere. I thought I might be able to seize the moment and sneak away, but Rodrigo stopped me.

"Don't you want to stay for the main event, *compadre?*" he said, pointing his automatic at my chest.

Rafael finished cutting up Mike and shoved the body parts off the table.

"Look, he takes up less space now," he said, grinning. "Bring me the other one."

Rodrigo and the Malian shoved me over the bloody floor toward Rafael. The boss turned me around, and his two helpers heaved me onto the table, which was sticky and slashed from the chainsaw. I felt as weak as a newborn.

"Wait, Ortega. What was the point of doing that little business with my Glock if you were just going to get rid of us this way?"

The Spaniard lifted the visor of his mask and gave me a faux-reflective look. "Well, if the police ever find your bodies—which I highly doubt they will—they'll think you killed each other."

"So, after gunning down Mike, I killed myself with a chainsaw?"

"It's true—the version that you put a bullet in your brain because you were wracked with guilt after killing your lover is more believable…"

He lowered his visor again, and the chainsaw purred.

"But that would deprive me of the pleasure of seeing what you're made of. In the literal sense, of course."

The chainsaw neared my midsection. I tensed and cried out. But before my scream could even bounce off the ceiling, a round of bullets from an automatic cracked in the air. Rafael stopped, his face dumbstruck, and placed the chainsaw on the ground. Rodrigo and the Malian, in turn, dropped their weapons and raised their hands. Someone was shouting behind me.

"Get down! On the ground! Now!"

I turned to see Rony coming at us, a Kalashnikov aimed at my would-be killers.

31

The cops showed up a few minutes after Rony. I wondered if he had alerted them just before stepping in. And now I was sitting in the back of an ambulance with a grimy blanket draped over my shoulders. The door was open, and my legs were dangling out. Deep in dark thoughts, I didn't notice Hamidou Kansaye walking toward me.

"So, Solo, looks like you almost got turned into sausage."

The commissioner had a satisfied look on his face. I couldn't tell if it was because I had been taught a lesson or because I had emerged in one piece from my near-death experience.

"'Almost' is the operative word, Commissioner."

I watched as Rafael Ortega and his accomplices, all of them in handcuffs, were led to a police van. Ortega turned to look at me, and we stared at each other for an interminably long moment.

"We're gonna lock that demon up in a cage, and his sidekicks too. My phone hasn't stopped ringing. Everyone wants the details, so tell me what happened."

In a monotone, I recounted my horrific night. I explained that Rafael Ortega was most likely the boss of a drug-trafficking ring and that Mike Kedzia was a straw man—a dispensable bookkeeper.

"You should look up Kedzia's prints. His hand should still be on the floor in there. I have a hunch that's not his real name. The others called him Alejandro. I'm guessing he's South American."

Kansaye nodded. "I already got a call from the prime minister's chief of staff ordering me to release Ortega. He's vouching for the Spaniard."

I closed my eyes and shook my head.

"Don't worry, I won't give in to any pressure. This case will be pursued all the way to the end. So, these paramedics are taking you to the emergency room to run some tests and—"

"How did you know?"

"Know what?"

"Where to find me."

The commissioner pointed to the large man standing off to the side. "Ask him."

Rony stepped up, his Gauloise hanging from his mouth. Kansaye took his leave, wishing me a speedy recovery.

"How'd you do it?" I asked the muscleman.

He pointed toward my loaned Land Cruiser in front of the slaughterhouse.

"I attached a GPS tracker to it. I didn't trust you."

I shook his hand a very long time.

"That was a fucking good idea," I said.

"I followed you in my old ride from the house to this place, and once I saw things were turning sour, I called the cops."

To think that I had wanted to be rid of him just a few hours earlier.

"If it weren't for you, I'd be crocodile food right about now."

"I couldn't let that happen. Poor animals. They're practically extinct as it is."

I belly laughed until my ribs hurt, a welcome reminder that I was alive.

The ambulance took me to Gabriel-Touré Hospital, where I was diagnosed with cracked ribs, a broken nose, and a slight concussion. They admitted me for observation, and needless to say, I slept like a baby, despite the comings and goings of the nurses.

~ ~ ~

The next morning, I called a cab to drive me home. It took me five minutes to get in the vehicle and about as much time to get out. I hobbled to the gate like an old man and rang the bell. Modibo's face lit up when he saw me. He gave me a big hug, which almost made me feel good.

"Boss, you're back," he said, squeezing me with his puny arms. "I'm so happy."

"Careful, kid. Every part of me hurts."

He inspected my puffy face.

"You don't look good at all."

He took me by the hand and carefully led me to my armchair on the patio. With a sigh of relief, I settled in. The kid vanished, and I watched the river and its somber waters while a flock of big-beaked hornbills weaved through the air. I was in pain, but I was alive.

Modibo returned with a glass of Scotch, neat. I thanked him, but he had already slipped away to give me my space. Deep down, I didn't think he was such a bad kid—even if he didn't drink. Rony showed up, and I offered him a whisky, but he didn't want to join me either.

"I came by to ask if you'd like me to stick around."

I reflected for a moment. "You'd be wasting your time. Those guys are behind bars. I'm no longer in danger."

Rony nodded. "All right then, I'll let you be. If you need anything, don't hesitate to ask. I'm leaving the Land Cruiser. It belongs to Milo. You can discuss the details with him."

He said good-bye and turned to leave.

"Rony," I called.

"Yes?"

"Thanks."

He looked at me with his black eyes.

"Don't mention it."

A man of few words.

That afternoon, despite my aches and pains and some dizziness, I went for a walk on the riverbank. I followed the meandering path as I retraced my thoughts. Up ahead, there was a Bozo fishing village. It was nothing more than a pile of huts made of mud-brick—banco. They were relics that would eventually yield to the relentless march of progress. I passed the fishermen who were bringing in their nets while others were unloading sand collected from the riverbed. That same sand would be used in the ugly buildings cropping up like mushrooms in the city. By collecting it, the Bozos were contributing to their own extinction. Fucking irony. I often wondered if they were aware of this, but knew deep down they were screwed anyway. When life is that hard, only the present matters. Tomorrow is a battle, and you aren't even sure you'll be around to meet it.

I watched them do their unforgiving work, their gnarly muscles glistening in the dangerously hot sun. Noticing my presence, they stopped to stare at me, but not with animosity.

I greeted them. "*Ani kilé.*"

Their sweaty faces lit up. "*M'ba, ani kilé. I ka kéné?*"

They were asking me how I was and appeared to be genuinely interested, which seemed incredible to me, a Westerner in part, so accustomed to offering such salutations only out of habit.

"*Toroo sitè.*"

They smiled and got back to work without forgetting to wave good-bye. Just beside them, women were washing their laundry in the current and stretching it out to dry on the bank. Suddenly, a flock of snot-nosed kids in tattered clothes surrounded me, pulling my sleeves and bombarding me with questions, which posed a threat to my basic level of Bambara. They followed me for a bit of the way, then got bored and scurried off, shrieking in high-pitched voices.

I looked out at the water. I was in pain, but I was alive.

32

The next day, Kansaye called to tell me that my hunch was right. They had run Mike Kedzia's fingerprints through Interpol, and a match had come up. His real name was Alejandro Hilario Nuñez, and he was originally from Colombia. He had been convicted in Spain on charges of laundering money from the trafficking of Colombian cocaine, and it had cost him two years in an Iberian prison. His uncle was a man named Tomas Nuñez, a leader of the Norte del Valle cartel. As for the dandy, his real name was, indeed, Rafael Ortega de la Torres. The Spaniard was once a high-ranking police officer. He lost his job after being implicated in a drug case in Malaga. Last but not least, the hidalgo who was now minus an ear was a Venezuelan. His full name was Rodrigo Camacho, and he hadn't been on Interpol's radar. I thanked the commissioner for keeping me in the loop.

"What are you going to do now?" he asked.

I realized he was worried. He didn't want me stirring up any more shit, and he was hoping I'd find some satisfaction in knowing that Rafael and his cohorts would be spending some time in prison. But he knew me all too well.

"I have a couple of things to check out."

There was silence on the other end of the call. Finally, Kansaye spoke. "Don't try anything without consulting me first. You got that, *Warakalan*?"

"I have one last favor to ask of you, sir. Could you keep the information about Mike Kedzia's true identity a secret? It's very important to me."

Kansaye had no problem with that. I promised I wouldn't do anything dangerous without his approval, and I'd keep him up to speed on my investigation. Semi-reassured, he ended the call. I went into my bedroom and grabbed my sleeping bag. I threw a change of clothes, some toiletries, a pair of binoculars, and my Glock, along with two magazines, into an old travel duffle. As incredible as it seemed, Kansaye had returned my weapon. It was of no use to him, as there were no ballistics labs in Mali. And that worked for me. The phone rang just as I was zipping up the duffle bag. It was Farah Tebessi. I really didn't want to answer.

Finally, I decided to pick up. "What do you want?" I asked.

"Can we meet?"

I was silent for several seconds. "When?"

"Now, if you can."

I hung up and threw the phone on my bed.

~ ~ ~

With a dry throat but clear mind, I knocked on the door of her room at the Laïco Hotel. She opened it a crack and looked at me through the small opening.

"Are you going to act like a gentleman this time?"

"That's not what you should expect from me."

She opened the door anyway.

"You look like crap."

"Thanks."

"Do you want a drink?"

I watched her walk over to the minibar as I sat down in a comfortable armchair. She was wearing a snug T-shirt and booty shorts that showed off the bottom of her bronze, perfectly round cheeks. Her ass was big, the way I liked them. And her legs were muscular.

"Scotch, neat. Thanks."

She emptied a miniature bottle into a whiskey glass and took out a diet cola for herself. She sat cross-legged on the bed and eyed me coldly as I took a sip.

"You didn't kill them," she said.

"As it turns out, eliminating a gang of heavily armed drug dealers is harder than you'd think."

"I'm not criticizing you. I'm just a little disappointed."

"Not as disappointed as I am," I said, thinking of Mike Kedzia—or rather, Alejandro Nuñez.

She rolled her icy glass along the inside of her thigh, leaving a trail of goose bumps.

"Now that they're behind bars, you'll drop the case, won't you?"

"No."

The Scotch did me good, but the room was getting hot. She hadn't turned on the AC, and I was sweating.

"What do you plan to do?"

"I'm going to pursue a couple of leads. This whole thing is unclear."

"What do you mean? It's so obvious. Bahia discovered their ploy, and as soon as she was released from custody, they killed her so she wouldn't talk."

"Over the years, I've learned to be suspicious of the obvious."

I downed the rest of the amber liquid, which burned my throat, and stood up.

"You don't want to stay?"

Yes, I wanted to stay. I was dying to stay, to drown myself in her body. I wanted to fuck her until I didn't have a drop of semen left. I wanted to forget how lonely I was.

"No."

I headed toward the door.

"Why?"

I turned around, my fingers on the handle.

"Why what?"

"They're in jail. They no longer pose a threat to you. Your friend will be avenged, and, in a way, Bahia will be too. So why keep going?"

"I don't know any other way."

I pressed down on the handle.

"Wait."

She got up and walked over to me. She put her hand on mine. We looked at each other suspiciously, like two enemies fascinated with each other—like lovers at war. I dominated her in height, but she had rendered me power-less with a simple touch. She took my hand and brought it to her breast. I grunted like an animal.

I was so weak, I just wanted her to take me.

I grabbed her, and my teeth banged hers as I kissed her with abandon. She pushed me back and slithered down my legs until she was on her knees—to better control me. She unzipped my fly and dropped my pants. Giving a small sigh at seeing how hard I was, she pulled my cock out of my boxers. She sucked me off, enjoying her total power over me.

I pulled away from her mouth so I wouldn't come too fast like an asshole, with my pants at my feet. I lifted her up, stumbled to the bed, and threw her on it. She looked at me with a victorious smile, her lips still wet from the blow job.

In a single move, I got rid of all my clothes. I was now standing before her fully naked, my dick tense like a bow, arrow engaged, my pants, shirt, underwear, and socks scattered lifelessly on the floor around me. To remove her shorts, I flipped her on her stomach like a sack of dirty laundry. She protested as I unceremoniously ripped off the skimpy piece of cloth. Then, fully aroused, I overcame her, thrusting myself between her yearning thighs. Her cry of pain turned into groans of pleasure as I repeatedly pushed deep into her. I squeezed her ass and chest to the point of bruising. I was starving for her. I turned her on her back and sank my head into her magnificent pussy. I devoured her and then I lapped her up. She twisted and moaned as my tongue searched her out and licked her over and over.

I hated her for wanting her so bad.

So I took her again, and as I came like a soldier surrendering his arms, she let out a teasing laugh. I buried myself in the sheets, conquered beyond hope.

~ ~ ~

Later, submerged in a sweaty stupor, I resisted the temptation to fall asleep. I still had my pride, what there was of it.

We had engaged in several more rounds of furious fucking, possessed by pleasure, ready to drown, exhausted and slightly nauseated. Now she was nestled against me, her head in the hollow of my shoulder, and she was stroking my chest. If I hadn't known who she was, I could have pictured something else—sappy bullshit.

"You're the first woman I've fucked in a long time who wasn't a whore," I said point blank. If I had wanted to hurt her, I got nothing for my trouble.

"Since your wife died?" she asked.

I closed my eyes and clenched my jaw. She rose up on her elbow and looked at me with a serious expression. Her big black eyes sparkled in the half-light.

"Say my name," she said.

"What?"

"I want you to say my name. That way, I'll know I'm real. And you'll know I'm real."

"What kind of bullshit—"

"Say it!"

"Farah. There, are you happy?"

"Again. Say it again."

So I said her name several more times, each time louder than the last. Before long, I was shouting it. When I stopped, there was a heavy silence between us. We looked at each other, and then I exploded in laughter. So did she. We laughed until we cried.

33

The next day, I got behind the wheel of my loaned Land Cruiser and hit the road. It was dawn, but the night was lingering. Stars were still twinkling high in the sky as the sun rose. Heading north, I crossed Martyrs Bridge and drove up Avenue Modibo-Keïta and then Avenue de la Liberté. Following the curves that snake along the Koulouba hill, I could see the beautiful and sleepy city down below. Street lamps were going out one after another. I passed the presidential palace on my left and headed toward Kati, which I crossed through after passing its military camp. I turned west and drove all the way to the town of Kita with the windows down and a cigarillo hanging from my mouth. There, I stopped at a service station to fill up. I didn't know if I'd be coming across another one before reaching Keniéba, and I didn't want to risk getting stranded in scrubland. I made a second stop at a small grocery store to buy mineral water and mangos. I put everything in the back, next to a foam mattress, which I had brought as a precaution. After stretching my legs, I got back on the road. To the north, the Mandingues Plateau and its sandstone cliffs towered over the road with their violet and rocky walls.

By late morning, I had reached the town of Bafing Makana, the capital of the Bafing National Park, south of the Manantali Reservoir. There were no tarred roads beyond this boondock town. I had to take a rough road full of *fech fech*—a white sand so fine, you could sink into it if you took your foot off the gas. I drove through a thick forest and arrived at the gravelly bank of a wide river. Some kids were waiting there for cars to come by. They surrounded the Land Cruiser, claiming they knew how to ford the river. I gave a one-thousand-franc bill to the boy who was clearly the oldest, and he led me into the current, which came up to his thighs. Thanks to them, I was able to cross without issue and head toward Kenieba. The temperature, which was comfortable at the beginning of the day, was now spiking, so I turned on the AC. I passed several heavy-equipment vehicles and SUVs with mining company names on them, but none sporting Cartagena's logo. As I drove, I observed the huge holes that had been dug into the sides of the Bambouk Mountains—gold mining exploits.

I arrived in Keniéba by midafternoon. I got more supplies and stopped at a *dibiterie*, a meat stand on the main street, to buy some greasy roasted goat. I ate it quickly and then went to the police station, where I asked an officer for directions to Cartagena's mines. The cop thought long and hard. Unable to answer my question, he went outside and asked an old man on the street, who was also stumped.

"Do you have an address?" the cop asked as he came back inside.

I recalled the name Dioulafondou from the Cartagena website. The officer's face lit up.

"Yes, I know that town. It's about thirty kilometers northeast of here. You have to take that dirt road over there," he said, pointing to a miserable path meant for donkeys and carts.

"That dirt road? Is it suitable for cars?"

The officer assured me it was. I thanked him, climbed into the Land Cruiser, and started down the dirt road. My cracked ribs were immediately begging for mercy, but I clenched my jaw while keeping my eyes peeled for obstacles. An hour and a half of ball-busting bumps later, I arrived in Dioulafondou. It was nothing more than a miserable cluster of twenty or so banco huts. Again, I asked how to get to the Cartagena mine. Few of the villagers spoke my language, but one old man was able to tell me in choppy French that he didn't know the mine. I thought quickly and asked if there was a landing strip close to the village. The old man nodded vigorously and pointed west.

"Over there! The white men—they've made a site for small planes."

The man confirmed that it was possible to get there by car. I thanked him profusely and drove off. The sun had begun its descent. I checked my watch; it was almost five o'clock. I had two hours of sunlight left, tops. Driving in the dark on a road as bad as this was suicidal, but I was in an adventurous mood. I drove a good hour, jostled in all directions. Finally, I arrived at the landing strip, which was no more than a field that had been cleared with a pickax. Humbert had been a damned good pilot to land his old crate on this makeshift plot of land.

I stopped the Land Cruiser and got out. Walking along the runway, I saw that it ended at a forest. At that point, a path began. I returned to the SUV and pulled my gun from my bag. I slipped it into the holster under my safari jacket. I walked a short fifteen minutes through the trees, listening to the songs of tropical birds and the warning cries of monkeys. I arrived at a rocky overhang above a vast crater. The path ended in front of a hut made of shoddy planks and topped with a rippled tin roof. Under a small lean-to, there was a generator that looked perfectly maintained. I called out, my hand on my Glock. The door of the hut creaked, and an old man appeared. He was wearing shorts but no shirt. The man was thin, with a washboard-like chest and black as pitch. He resembled Drissa.

"*Ani oula,*" I said.

"*M'ba, ani oula,*" he replied, squinting.

"I'm looking for the Cartagena mine."

He looked at me suspiciously. "It's here."

I looked around.

"I'm sorry, but I don't see any mine."

He pointed at the crater down below.

"That's the mine."

I walked up to the edge.

As I peered over the rim, I could tell that the crater was man-made. Much of it was covered with vegetation, but I could still make out the tracks left by heavy vehicles.

"How long has it been since they've done any mining here?"

The old man scratched his head.

"To be honest, I can't remember. Must be a good twenty years."

"And what about you? What are you doing here?" I asked.

"Me? I watch over the mine, and I pass mail along to Bamako when the plane comes once a month."

~ ~ ~

I kept talking to the watchman without paying attention to the setting sun. When I noticed the old man's shadow stretching to infinity like a Giacometti sculpture, I realized it was time to go. I thanked him and started hurrying back to my car. When I got there, night had fallen. The forest echoed with nocturnal animal cries, and the trees felt as though they were swaying. I had the sensation of being on an old ocean vessel. I debated getting back on the road but quickly abandoned the idea. I had a fifty-fifty chance of breaking something important. So I got out the foam mattress and set it up on the roof of the SUV. I unrolled my sleeping bag. Above me, the nighttime sky was covered with a fiery carpet of stars. Under the shooting stars, I savored juicy sweet slices of mangos, which I ate right off the blade of my pocket knife, ecstatic as a kid.

34

I am so scared.

They are there, both of them —on stretchers.

The medical examiner hasn't come in yet. He must be torturing some other body in some other exam room, trying to extract the truth behind its passing. I have been in this room with its white tiles so many times, but it has never felt this cold before. I shiver. I walk toward them without really realizing it. My feet don't seem to be touching the floor.

Next to their bodies, clear plastic bags hold their personal belongings, most likely collected by the paramedics. Among their things is the tagelmust I gave my wife early in our marriage. I had bought it from a Tuareg guy at the Marché de Médine in Bamako. I pull it out. It's stained with blood. *Her* blood. I bury my face in the piece of cloth and quietly sob, taking in the scent of a citrusy perfume. *Her* perfume. It mingles with the metallic odor of death. Slipping the chèche under my jacket, I step closer. They are still inside the body bags.

One small, one big.

I dry my tears and unzip the big bag part of the way. Through the opening, I can see her face. One eye is open and the other closed in an unholy beyond-the-grave wink. I close the open eye and gently brush her cold cheek. She almost looks likes she's sleeping—if it weren't for the blood under her nose and at the corner of her mouth.

I unzip the bag all the way.

She's wearing hardly any clothes. The first responders had cut them off when they were trying to save her. They always did that. I look at her pale nakedness under the humming fluorescent lights. I stroke her glacial skin again. I can't recognize the woman I loved in this body, the body I knew as though it were my own. The sagging breasts I had kneaded with passion. The pussy I had petted, licked, and penetrated while whispering dirty things. I loved her so much and betrayed her in so many ways. I inch closer, inspecting her fine features, which death hasn't managed to make any less beautiful. I'm looking for something—I don't know what. A residual trace of her soul, a spark. Something. But there is nothing, nothing but corroded flesh and dusty bones. I picture flies laying eggs. I close my eyes and open them again. I look at my hand and notice a vein in my wrist pulsating to the irregular beat of my dying heart.

Crying now, I walk over to the small bag. I seethe with hatred and despair, not knowing which one will win. I suspect it will be hatred. With me, hate always has the last word.

My hand trembling and my eyes closed, I unzip the bag. Eventually I open my eyes—and roar like a beast.

35

The chirping of rowdy birds woke me at sunrise. Still grog-
gy, I watched a female warthog digging with her little
ones at the edge of the forest. I rolled up my foam mattress
and sleeping bag and got back on the road. I returned
the way I had come, crossing through Dioulafondou and
veering toward Keniéba. My loyal housekeeper, Modibo,
was waiting when I arrived home after hours of driving.
Barely out of the car, I was subjected to an assault of kindness. The kid grabbed my bag and took it to my room.
Then he followed me like a puppy, giving me updates on
the house, the neighborhood, and the entire city as if I had
been gone for a month. Exhausted, I told him he was done
for the day, and he definitely looked hurt. Watching him
leave without saying a word, I felt guilty.

Lost in thought, I had dinner alone.

The next morning, I had my coffee on the patio. Modibo
waited on me—in silence for the first time. Ironically, it
bothered me that he wasn't saying anything.

Filthy kid.

My phone rang. It was Kansaye.

"Solo, I have bad news. Very bad news, indeed," he said,
skipping the preliminaries.

I already knew what he was going to say.

"They're going to be released. They bought off the judge and probably the entire tribunal. I'm mad as hell."

"They've got the dough."

"I ranted and raved, Solo. I made threats. It was no use. Rafael and Rodrigo are going to be released tomorrow morning."

"That's perfect."

For a second, I actually thought he had lost his voice.

"What do you mean, *that's perfect*? These guys will be bent on finishing the job. It's all systems go."

All systems go. Kansaye tried so hard, but he always wound up being so unhip. I was glad he couldn't see me, because I was smiling.

"It's perfect for my needs. For what I have planned, they have to be released. And despite what you say, I doubt I'm a priority."

Kansaye subjected me to a barrage of reminders about being careful, and I promised I'd call on my bodyguard again if things took a downturn. I ended the conversation and entered the French embassy's number. I asked to speak with the security attaché. I waited a few moments, listening to interminable recorded music, and finally someone picked up.

"Yes?"

"Hello, sir."

"Hello. To whom am I speaking?"

"We met recently at a small party at the ambassador's residence. This is Souleymane Diabaté. You know, the griot…"

There was an icy silence.

"Camara. What do you want?"

"I need a favor."

"You've got some nerve, asshole."

"I'm not coming to you empty-handed."

"Go fuck yourself."

"Would a huge coke haul be of interest to you?"

Another round of silence. I knew I had him. A delectable drug seizure—that always made the pigs salivate. They couldn't do anything about it. It was in their genes.

"Let's meet at the Kempinski El Farouk hotel. At the bar. In half an hour."

Satisfied, I ended the call.

"Modibo!" I called. "You ride a Jakarta, right?"

~ ~ ~

The Kempinski El Farouk hotel was built on concrete pillars alongside the Niger River. I strode through the luxurious lobby as I headed to the bar, which overlooked the river's brown waters. Drinking orange juice through a straw, the attaché was waiting for me at a table. I pulled out a chair across from him.

"Thank you for granting me a bit of your time," I said as I sat down.

"Talk to me about the cocaine," he said, scowling.

"You've heard about the chainsaw murder?"

"Obviously."

"I was there when it happened."

"What? That's not mentioned anywhere in the Malian police reports!"

I waved the waiter over and ordered a coffee.

"I owe that to the kindness of the police commissioner."

The French cop studied me.

"I would like to know why the all-powerful police com-missioner is protecting a fugitive."

"My father and he were childhood friends. They grew up together. For a Malian, families of the heart are just as important as families by blood. They carry all the same obligations. Kansaye is a father figure. He looks out for me."

"I see. Getting back to this coke, I'd like to know more. Why did the Malians cover up your involvement?"

The waiter placed a cup of coffee in front of me.

"I'm not involved. I'm working a case as a private inves-tigator on behalf of a client. Conducting my investigation, I ended up crossing paths with a ring of drug traffickers. I was very close to suffering the same fate as that poor guy."

"Mike Kedzia."

"You're up to speed."

"On the phone, you said you were seeking a favor."

"I need you to get in touch with a certain Latin American liaison officer."

The attaché looked at me indifferently. "And what do I get out of it?"

"I'll share all the information I uncover. A huge deal is about to go down—a delivery, I'm assuming."

The attaché burst out laughing. "Well, well, well."

"Inspector, what do you have to lose? I know more about this case than anyone else. And to prove my word is good, I'll give you a piece of intel that will be of great interest to your colleagues in Paris."

"Let's hear it."

"The Ukrainian—Mike Kedzia—is actually Colombian. His real name's Alejandro Hilario Nuñez."

The French attaché remained stone-faced, but I had a feeling that he was bubbling with excitement.

"Okay, we have an agreement," he said, clearing his throat. "What exactly would you like me to ask this liaison officer?"

I told him and was happy to see his eyes widen in surprise.

36

When Rafael and Rodrigo exited the jail in the late morning, I was waiting patiently, straddling Modibo's Chinese moped. There's no better way to blend in. Thousands of the two-wheelers vroom through the streets of Bamako. For the occasion, I was wearing a pair of torn jeans and an old T-shirt. My helmet bore the insignia of an AIDS NGO. An enormous pair of shades covered half my face. I was unrecognizable, to say the least. A small door in the enormous metal gate opened, and the two Hispanic men emerged. Blinded by the sun, they shielded their eyes while scanning the area. I turned away instinctively, even though they couldn't recognize me. Rodrigo, who was still bandaged, gave the jailer a hearty handshake while Rafael waved to the Pajero parked in the shade on the small square across from the jail. Coulibaly was behind the wheel. He started the car and pulled up in front of his new bosses. I couldn't blame him—he did have a family to feed. Rafael and Rodrigo got in the SUV, and it began heading in the direction of the river. I followed suit, sidling into the heavy pre-lunch-hour traffic. We hadn't driven that far—about half a mile—when the Pajero stopped in front of the Apaloosa, a Tex-Mex restaurant famous for its Ukrainian hostesses and waiters in ridiculous cowboy hats.

After surviving on a jail diet, my drug traffickers needed an appetizing lunch. Coulibaly dropped off his passengers and got back on the road. I parked my bike a short distance from the restaurant, next to a cigarette stand in the shade of a mango tree. The vendor and I made casual conversation about the situation in the North and the Tuareg separatists who were in the news after attacking a police station in Kidal. The vendor offered me some tea. Even though we were under the tree, the sun was beating down on us. It was the worst time of day, when you feel like a melting stick of butter, when you drown in your own sweat. I imagined my Hispanics living it up in the cool breeze of the Apaloosa's AC. I waited three hours, and soon the cigarette seller and I had run out of things to say. We stood there like that, the silence interrupted only by customers seeking counterfeits of well-known American cigarettes.

I was relieved to see the Pajero pull up around three o'clock. It wasn't long before Rafael and Rodrigo came out of the Apaloosa and slid into the car. I said good-bye to the cigarette vendor and took off after the SUV. It stopped in front of a big villa in the ACI-2000 neighborhood, which I assumed was their crash pad. After spending several hours in the villa, they emerged in the early evening, showered, shaved, and sporting clean clothes. My tailgating then led me down Avenue Kassé Keïta, near the train station. The Pajero parked in a lot in front of the French oil company Total. I did the same, slipping on the kind of face mask motorcyclists often wear to protect themselves from exhaust fumes. I got off the Jakarta and pulled a manila envelope I had prepared out of the satchel. I watched as Rafael and his crew emerged from the Pajero and headed toward an old security guard in an impeccable brown uniform who was manning the entrance. I followed them.

"We have a meeting with Mr. Ibrahim Soumano," Rafael announced while Rodrigo scanned the area. He turned around and saw me.

I started to sweat, but I didn't look away. I grabbed a ballpoint pen in my pocket and scribbled on the envelope as Rodrigo stared at me indifferently.

"Second floor, fourth door on the right," the guard told the men.

They walked off and began climbing the stairs to the second floor. Now it was my turn. I removed my mask and approached the guard. "I have a delivery for Mr. Ibrahim Soumano," I told him, showing him the envelope on which I had just scribbled the name.

"He's in a meeting. But you can leave the envelope here if you wish. I'll make sure he gets it."

I tried to look upset.

"That doesn't work for me. My boss instructed me to deliver it personally. It's very important."

"Then you'll just have to wait. Second floor, fourth door on the right."

I thanked him and followed his directions. I waited a good half hour at the door, and when Rafael and Rodrigo came out, I turned my back. As soon as they disappeared down the hall, I knocked.

"Come in."

I walked into the nicely cooled office. A guy wearing a plaid button-down and a filthy purple tie was staring at me from behind a pair of glasses with thick lenses. His messy desk was piled high with papers, as were all the shelves and most of the chairs. The guy's office was a temple dedicated to the pencil-pusher gods.

"What do you want?" he asked in the impatient tone bureaucrats use to assert their importance.

I threw the envelope in his wastebasket and flashed a fake police badge.

"Inspector Souleymane Camara from the criminal investigations unit," I declared pompously, praying he wouldn't recognize me.

"What do you want, Inspector?"

Clearly, I wasn't as famous as I thought I was.

"I'm investigating the two men who just left your office."

"Mr. Ortega and his associate are highly successful and respected businessmen," Soumano protested, as if I had implicated him personally.

"You're right. That's when they're not playing with their chainsaws."

"I beg your pardon. Mr. Ortega and his associate have been exonerated of any wrongdoing in that case."

"I would like to know why they came to speak with you."

Soumano looked at me suspiciously.

"You may be a police investigator, but why they were here is none of your business. As I said, they've been ex-onerated of any wrongdoing and released from jail. Don't you need a warrant or a formal request for this kind of information?"

"You're wasting my time. Call my boss, Chief of Police Pierre Diawara. He'll back me up."

I gave him the number, and because he was hesitating, I really drove it home.

"Hurry up, or would you prefer a little visit from the entire criminal investigation unit!" I thundered.

My order, delivered with all the confidence I had man-aged to summon, produced the desired effect. Soumano did what I told him to do. He slowly entered the number on his landline and pressed the speakerphone button. The receptionist answered, and Soumano asked to speak with the chief. When I heard Pierre pick up, my heart tightened. I didn't know how he would react.

"Chief, I have one of your men here with me: Inspector Souleymane Camara. He claims to be looking into a few of our clients. He has an unusual request. That's why I would like you to confirm that he is, indeed, working for you as an undercover investigator."

There was a pause on the other end of the line. I started to sweat. Finally, Pierre spoke.

"Inspector Camara is a highly regarded member of our team. I suggest that you respond to every one of his requests."

Soumano gave a forced smile.

"Very well, Chief."

"Solo, can he hear me?"

"Yes, indeed. You're on speakerphone."

"Please keep me up to speed on the progress of your very important investigation."

"I certainly will, Chief."

Soumano hung up. "What do you need, Inspector? We'll be happy to help you in any way."

I sat down in a chair, stretched out my legs, and put my hands behind my head. My insolent attitude hardly raised an eyebrow.

"I need to know the reason for Ortega's visit."

Soumano cleared his throat. All of this was hard for him to swallow.

"Mr. Ortega and his associate came to make sure their requested delivery is being processed and will arrive on time."

"And is it?"

"Yes, it is."

We looked at each other in silence for several long seconds.

"And? What is this delivery?"

He sighed, and I actually thought he was going to cry.

"A tanker truck filled with Jet A."

"And what is Jet A?"

"Kerosene. It's airplane fuel."

37

As I rode back home on the Jakarta, I thought about what Soumano had said. Rafael was having Jet A delivered, and this fuel would only be used for jet planes. The two old crates that Stéphane Humbert piloted for Cartagena had traditional piston engines. So then, what plane was this fuel designated for? Just as I was beginning to form an idea, my phone went off inside my pocket, killing my train of thought. I answered while steering with one hand. Despite the danger factor of such a move, I was able to stay the course while talking to Pierre. He wanted to remind me of my promise to provide him with an explanation. I switched up my route and headed in the direction of the criminal investigations office.

After knocking back a couple of beers with Pierre, I explained how I was continuing my investigation of Cartagena. I had merely checked out a few remote possibilities. I had "closed off avenues," as those on the force put it. Pierre nodded, but I could tell he didn't believe me. He insisted that I report every piece of information I uncovered, whether it was extraneous or pertinent. I put my hand over my heart and swore I would, and as I left his office, I had a bad taste in my mouth. But I had decided not to bring him in on all of it. The coming days would be decisive. There could be collateral victims, as was the case with Bahia Tebessi. Too many innocent people had died already.

On the way home, I stopped at an electronics shop and picked up a satellite telephone with a car charger. Nothing worked better for making calls from the middle of nowhere. Outside the cities and major towns, cell coverage was sparse.

Back at the house, I treated myself to a relaxing cool shower and put on a pair of shorts, I went to inspect the Land Cruiser. It took me a good ten minutes to find Ronny's magnetic GPS tracker underneath the engine block, near the radiator. I pulled it off and examined the casing. It had a cable with a male USB port. I hooked it up to my computer and quickly figured out how to download the correct application. Fifteen minutes later, the GPS's location showed up on Google Earth. Satisfied, I charged the battery before going to bed.

The next morning, I awoke to the sound of the Muslim call to prayer and hopped in the shower to scrub off the remaining traces of my dreams. I packed my canvas bag with things I would need for a trip that would last no more than a week. I didn't know where this investigation would take me, but I wanted to be as prepared as possible. So I slipped my laptop with a heavy case into the bag, along with a pair of binoculars, my digital camera equipped with a telephoto lens, and the satellite phone. After a light and simple breakfast, I borrowed Modibo's Jakatar again and rode off toward the airport.

When I got there, I spotted huge fuel tanks bearing Total's logo in a storage area. I found a shady place to wait with the moped. Soumano was sure the delivery would take place in the morning. When I asked him how many times Ortega and his men had placed orders for Jet A, Four-Eyes checked on his computer, and I was stunned. This was the third time in a year.

The sun was already high in the sky, and the damned thing was moving along happily. The Harmattan trade winds were whipping up piping-hot clouds of dirt. Like an idiot, I hadn't thought to slip a bottle of water into one of the moped's satchels. My mouth was parched.

Before I could dwell on it, a tanker driven by Rodrigo pulled up. A Malian muscleman was in the passenger seat. It was the giant who was with him at the slaughterhouse. They drove right by me, oblivious to my presence, and pulled into a hydrocarbon stockroom. It took them an hour to load up the truck and sign the paperwork. When the vehicle left, I tailed it as it headed toward Bamako. We hit heavier traffic at the city's periphery, and I used the time at a red light to position myself behind the vehicle.

I glanced in the large outside mirror to make sure the Malian meathead wasn't looking my way. Seeing that I was still off their radar, I took out the magnetic GPS tracker from my safari jacket and stuck it underneath the right fender—a place it could be spotted only under close examination. It made a small clunking sound, but no one noticed. When the light turned green, the truck took off toward the Pont du Roi Fahd. I didn't follow. There was no need to suck up any more exhaust fumes. Back at the house, I plugged in my laptop and clicked on the GPS tracker icon. To my great relief, it was working perfectly and was indicating Cartagena's headquarters. Modibo came into the room with a chilled beer. I thanked him and downed it in just a few gulps.

~ ~ ~

When I awoke the next day, I rushed to my laptop. Shit! The tanker was on the move. It was heading toward the town of Segou to the east. Those fuckers had left in the night. I drank a quick cup of coffee, grabbed my travel bag, slid my Glock into its holster, and hopped into the SUV. After giving Modibo a few hasty instructions, I reassured him that I'd be back soon. The kid seemed disoriented, worried even.

"Don't fret. Everything will be all right," I told him.

He gave me a confused look.

"What does fret mean?"

An ocher cloud of dirt went whipping in the air as I sped off.

38

I threaded my way along Bamako's congested avenues. Without an Internet connection, I wouldn't be able to check the tracker until I got to the next town. But I wasn't worried, because in the direction the tanker was heading, there was only one route, and it led to Segou. I'd reassess the situation there. I smoked a cigarillo as I dodged the deep potholes and the squabbling kids. The air outside was already filthy and burning hot, like the gray cigarillo smoke filling the inside of my Land Cruiser. Finally I reached the suburbs on the other side of Bamako. I passed the bus station and the police department at the city limits and hit the gas, making the bleak Sahel plains slip out of sight more quickly.

I reached Segou in the late morning and stopped at the Auberge, a hotel-restaurant owned by an old Lebanese Christian. The place had excellent food. An employee pointed me to the lobby where I could get an Internet connection to check the tanker's location. I saw that it was also in Segou and I stopped on the main street about a quarter mile away. The driver was probably having lunch at the Indépendence, a competing hotel on the Rue Nationale. I settled into a chair by the pool and ordered shawarma and a refreshing glass of rosé. When I checked on the truck again, it was already on the move, heading southeast on the road leading to San and then northeast to Mopti. It was foolish to get on the road right away, at the risk of winding up directly behind my target, so I booked a room in the Auberge annex to play tourist for the rest of the day. I spent the afternoon wandering along the picturesque promenade that followed the Niger River. When nighttime came, a tremendous sunset hugged the horizon, painting the dark waters and mud homes shades of ocher and purple. I happily took in the calmness that fell upon Segou while I watched seamen unload sacks of rice and coal, pottery, red meat, and dry fish from their fishing vessels and carry them to the riverbank. As the sun disappeared into the calm waters of the river, I thought of Farah.

~ ~ ~

In the early morning, my eyes still heavy with sleep, I checked the GPS app. The tanker trunk was moving. The driver was leaving Mopti and heading in the direction of Douentza. After a quick shower, I ordered some coffee and fresh bread with baobab honey. After paying the bill and saying one last good-bye to the hotel owner, I got back on the road, feeling the tinge of heartache I experienced every time I left Segou. I drove all day, dodging the ruts in the road and the suicidal goats and giving wide berth to the packed buses traveling at breakneck speed. By noon, I had passed Djenne, with its distinctive adobe architecture. Situated between two branches of the Bani, a tributary of the Niger River, it was once an important trade center, but that was many centuries ago. I stopped in the small town of Sofara, where I replenished my supply of mineral water and purchased sardines and some white bread at a roadside stall. I ate directly from the tin as I sat beneath the shade of an old tree with a knotted trunk in a small square. I remedied my dehydration by drinking an entire bottle of water. I quickly became the object of attention of a group of idle kids and gave them the empty bottle. They thanked me in Bambara, convinced I was one of them.

By midafternoon, I had reached the crossroads town of Sevare, with Mopti to the west and Bandiagara and the Dogon region to the south. I took the route heading northeast, toward Douentza, and hit the gas because I was counting hard on reaching Hombori before nightfall.

I was entering the northern part of Mali, which the French embassy had declared a red zone. Expats were strongly discouraged from traveling in this unstable region, ruled by jihadists and traffickers of all sorts of contraband— cigarettes, weapons, drugs, and even humans. When it came to this modern-day Far West, Mali's security forces had no choice but to grin and bear it. Although they were expected to crack down, they didn't stand a chance against the gangs of traffickers who were better equipped and more driven. How could a few men in beat-up pickups go up against hundreds of well-armed thugs in brand-new SUVs? The few men who had the risky job of protecting the region were paid next to nothing anyway, so who could blame them for closing their eyes and taking a contemptuously offered wad of bills?

On the road, I passed a French military convoy of armored tanks in tactical formation. It made me think of *Mad Max*. These were special forces units with ultra-modern weaponry. They had been based in Sevare since the rise of al-Qaeda terrorist kidnappings in northern Mali. The elite French soldiers were offering the Malian army logistical aid and training, but no one was fooled. The French forces would be gone one day, and in all likelihood, the jihadists would sweep away the Malian forces like so much debris carried off by the Harmattan winds.

The Sahelian wasteland had ceded its place to a turbulent landscape of dangerously steep sandstone cliffs and scrubby scree. Vehicles were becoming sparser. Now I was passing caravans of indolent camels and the settlements of the Fula people, West Africa's nomadic herders who lived in domed grass dwellings that could be easily set up, taken down, and transported. Kids along the sides of the asphalt road waved enthusiastically at passing cars as they tried to hawk their meager supplies of charcoal, salt, and small toys that they had fashioned themselves. I stopped at a café in Douentza, the crossroads town between Gao and Timbuktu. I ordered tea and haggled with the owner, a money-grubbing Songhai man. His tiled cafe had the only Wi-Fi in town, and using his connection wound up costing me a thousand francs. I had no trouble tracing the route of my truck. It was heading in the direction of Gao.

By dusk I had reached Hombori, a village surrounded by mountains in the Gourma region. In the distance, I saw the silhouette of the Hand of Fatima, a massive rock formation with five fingerlike peaks. I found a hotel. A simple fan in my room did its best to keep the air moving and dry the sweat on my skin, but it wasn't up to the task. I spent the better part of the night standing in my doorway in boxers while chatting with some French rock climbers who had ignored the red-zone travel warning and were planning to scale the Hand of Fatima at dawn the following day. We drank beers and smoked some weed supplied by their guide.

39

When I got back on the road, I had an awful migraine and no pain relievers. I fought it, reminding myself that I had asked for this. Soon the craggy mountains of Gourma gave way to a rocky desert where scrawny goats and placid camels roamed.

I was in the Sahara.

By late morning, I had crossed the bridge that spanned the Niger River to Bilal Koyra. Gao was very close, only a few kilometers north. I drove along the dirt road that followed the river. Tuareg settlements were scattered along the sides of the road, but many of them had few, if any, residents. A drought was forcing families to abandon the settlements and seek refuge in the large towns.

Finally, I arrived on the outskirts of Gao. Once on the wide and partially sand-covered streets in the downtown area, I stopped at a service station to fill up the tank of the Land Cruiser. Then I set off to find a decent hotel near Gao's port neighborhood. I set my sights on the Atlantide, which I knew was well-kept and had air-conditioned rooms. I parked the SUV in a lot behind the establishment. Rafael and his accomplices knew my car, and I didn't want them spotting it. At the front desk, I paid for one night and followed the receptionist as she led me to my room. The sparse and unrefined décor consisted of local crafts for undemanding tourists, wooden sculptures, and bogolan wall hangings. But it was clean, and the AC worked. I took a quick shower and sat down on the bed with my computer. I connected to the hotel's wi-fi and was relieved to see that the tanker truck was parked not too far from me, near the Askia Hotel. I kept my laptop on and activated an alert to indicate when the vehicle started moving. That night, I ate at the hotel restaurant. I had an excellent fillet of *capitaine*—caught in the river the night before, according to my waiter—which was served with a flavorful white rice. I knocked back a couple of beers with some French hydrologists and returned to my room. I stayed cooped up there, as I didn't want to venture out and risk running into the drug traffickers in town. I slept fitfully until the alert went off. It was a few minutes past six. I rushed to get dressed.

~ ~ ~

The streets of Gao were still sleepy. The sun was rising listlessly, and women were tackling their first task of the day—making fires in their small cast-iron stoves. I drove past an animal market housing dozens of placid dromedaries. I easily found the road that the large truck had taken fifteen minutes earlier. It was heading northeast. Unfortunately, as soon as I left Gao, putting peddle to the metal, I started encountering one challenge after another. I swung the steering wheel from left to right and back again as I dodged the obstacles of nature thrown cunningly in front of my wheels—knotty tree stumps, hazardous holes, and unaware animals. I eased up on the gas to avoid a mechanical breakdown.

Apparently, the other trucks and cars on this arid steppe, peppered with withered bushes, bony trees, and sepia stones, were moving along slowly too, because half an hour later I found myself in a cloud of dust raised by a line of vehicles in front of me. That's when things got complicated. I couldn't follow the tracker, and I needed to know if I was still behind the crew. I had to locate them, and to do that, I had to veer off the road and get a good look at the impromptu caravan. I drove several yards in the sand and braked. I grabbed my binoculars from my backpack and brought them to my eyes. Because I was no longer in the line of traffic, the cloud of dust didn't bother me anymore. The tanker was, indeed, moving along the beat-up road, preceded by the Pajero. I stepped on the gas, and driving on the sand, I barreled past the vehicles that had been just ahead of me. Then I got back on the road, lit a cigarillo, and slowed down. All I had to do now was follow the tanker's cloud—at a respectful distance, of course.

I drove like that for six more hours, opting to go off-road every so often. Oddly enough, doing that at some points made for a smoother ride. Suddenly, the cloud of dust caved in like a failed soufflé. I drove a good hundred feet through the sand, praying that my car wouldn't sink into it. Finally, I stopped behind a thicket of shrubbery that appeared to be desperately determined to thrive. I figured I could hide the vehicle there. I grabbed my backpack and got out of the car.

When the heat hit me, I almost collapsed. I took small puffs of painfully hot air to get my lungs accustomed. Then I looked around. There was no other vegetation to conceal me. I crept forward with my head down. In front of me, I made out a slight elevation, which I headed toward. By the time I reached the base of the hill, I was dripping with sweat. I spread out in the white-hot sand and crawled like a fakir over a bed of embers until I reached the top. I got as comfortable as I could behind a large rock and tried to ignore the burning sand. When I looked over the edge, I saw a bizarre scene. Half a dozen vehicles were stopped near a rusty but clearly operational bulldozer. Among the other vehicles were the tanker, the Pajero, and four sand-colored pickups. Some men were in the midst of a discussion. I raised the binoculars to my eyes. Rodrigo and Rafael were talking to a Malian wearing a military officer's uniform. All around them were soldiers in combat uniforms. They were armed with AK-47s. One of them was working a .50-caliber machine gun mounted on a tripod in the back of one of the pickups.

One other detail caught my attention. I adjusted the binoculars to bring them into the sharpest focus possible. Painted on the side of the vehicle with the machine gun was the emblem of the Malian National Guard. I put down the binoculars and spent the next few seconds cursing between my teeth. So Rafael and Rodrigo were in cahoots with the National Guard. I took out my camera and played with the telephoto lens until I had the focus I needed. I took a photo of Rafael and his accomplices, the soldiers, and their vehicles. Right beside the vehicles I noticed a wide, flat surface a few hundred feet long. On both sides, it was lined with huge rocks and rusty barrels. A landing strip. I took a picture of it.

Still crouched at my observation post, I watched as three luxury V8 Land Cruisers with tinted windows and Niger license plates pulled up alongside the Hispanics and the Malian. Seven men, fierce- and professional-looking Arabs in black shades, stepped out of the vehicles. They were wearing Pataugas boots and safari pants, and they were all armed with American AR-15 assault weapons. They formed a circle around the SUVs, and then one of them knocked on the back window of the vehicle in the middle. A door opened, and a man who appeared to be in his sixties emerged. He was North African, plump like Buddha, with fly-away hair and a jet-black mustache. I took his picture as he gave Rafael a hearty handshake and the Malian officer saluted him respectfully. Quickly, they entered into an animated conversation. I noticed that the Spanish ex-cop was glancing impatiently at his watch. Rodrigo walked up to him and handed him a satellite phone. The drug trafficker spoke a few words into the receiver and gave it back to Rodrigo.

That's when I heard it. An almost undetectable sound that grew louder. A jet engine. I scanned the sky, but saw nothing. Down below, Rafael was pointing toward something in the west, and the Buddha and the military officer were following his finger. Feverishly, I placed the camera atop my bag and aimed my binoculars in the direction he was pointing. And I saw it, coming closer from the west, the nose of a shiny aircraft shimmering in the heat.

40

The aircraft was a trijet, an older model. Although my aviation knowledge was limited, I guessed it was a Boeing 727. I watched as the landing gear dropped and the ailerons and flaps engaged. Practically at a crawling speed, the plane got into position on the runway's centerline, whipping up a gigantic dust cloud. Its nose came down, and the wheels touched the makeshift track. The engines roared as the pilot switched into reverse thrust to decelerate. Thick smoke rose in the burning heat, and the plane shook so much you'd think it had Parkinson's. I was highly skeptical of the runway's sufficiency, but the 727 eventually stopped at the very edge of it, in front of a row of small dunes. One of the Buddha's men spoke into a portable radio, and immediately a dozen pickups carrying Arab men in tagelmusts arrived out of nowhere. Some of them had Kalashnikov rifles over their shoulders. They parked near the baggage hold of the plane, whose engines continued to turn.

Rafael and his cohorts started walking toward the plane as the door near the pilot's cabin opened. A man with brown hair stuck his head out. He lowered a ladder and climbed down while Rodrigo held it in place. Two more men came out the same way. The 727 pilot and his team gave Rafael and Rodrigo a warm greeting and shook hands with the Buddha and the Malian officer. The Arabs jumped out of their pickups and opened the doors of the baggage hold. Then they went to work unloading the plane's cargo. They formed a human chain, passing bundles wrapped in plastic from hand to hand to the backs of the trucks, where they were carefully stacked. There were hundreds of bundles. Several tons of merchandise—no doubt cocaine. It was probably the same stuff that Bahia Tebessi had the bad luck of transporting. In shock over this discovery, I didn't notice the soldiers right away. But then I couldn't miss them. They were shouting to each other and gesturing wildly in my direction.

Shit! Motherfucking shit!

How the hell did they spot me? Then I realized my massive mistake. My camera lens. It was reflecting the sunlight. What a dumbass I was! A fucking amateur. I had revealed my spot by sending shiny signals in their direction. Three guards jumped into the back of the pickup with the machine gun. The truck spewed sand as it revved up and headed straight at me. I turned around to see if I could get to my SUV in time. It was too far away. And besides, the machine gun would turn it into a smoking carcass in no time. I rummaged anxiously in the backpack beside me. I took out the satellite phone and, with trembling fingers, punched in a number. The pickup was getting closer. It was slowing down, and the men in the back were fiercely scanning the terrain. The phone kept sounding one ring after another, and I could tell the voice mail would soon pick up.

Answer the fucking phone!

"Yes?" I heard Kansaye's sullen voice at the other end of the call.

"Commissioner, it's Solo," I said quickly. "Listen carefully. In a few seconds, I'm going to get captured by the
National Guard, units from Gao. They'll kill me if you
don't step in real fast."

I ended the call and snatched the memory card from
my camera. The pickup was now several yards from me. I
swiftly slipped my pants down, shoved the memory card in
my rectum, and pulled my pants back up. The Arab with
the machine gun tapped on the roof of the vehicle while
yelling something in Tamasheq, the Tuareg language
spoken around Timbuktu. The truck hurtled forward, its
wheels stopping centimeters from my feet. Sand flew all
over me. I stood up, spitting out a mouthful of the grit
and gingerly opening my eyes. The men jumped out of
the vehicle and pointed their rifles at my chest. I raised my
hands in surrender.

41

Rafael and Rodrigo grinned as the guards chucked me from the truck, tied up like a roast. The sand didn't do much to cushion the fall. I hit the ground with a groan.

"Mr. Camara, how wonderful to see you again," the Spaniard said.

"The feeling's not mutual, you sack of shit."

Rodrigo walked closer, his hand on his weapon.

"So, fatty, how are the neck and the ear?" I said, sniggering. "Not infected, I hope."

The Venezuelan drew his Beretta.

"Wait!"

The Buddha had come over, accompanied by the National Guard officer, a colonel, judging by the stripes on his shoulder.

"What's going on here? Who is this man?"

Rafael glanced at the soldiers, who were tensing up, and at the Arab bodyguards, whose rifles were at the ready. He relaxed his shoulders in an effort to calm himself.

"Nobody... He's nobody, just a nuisance. A private detective who's been snooping in our business. We'll fix that right away.

"Don't believe any of that, General," I sneered. "Killing me would be counterproductive."

The Buddha went white. "What makes you think I'm a general?"

I knew I was being way too cocky, but I had to gain some time any way I could.

"They may be wearing civilian clothes, but your men are clearly soldiers. Besides, the colonel here gave you a respectful military salute. From that I deduced, you're a rank above him, which would make you a general. I'm leaning toward Algeria's military. The Nigerien plates on your vehicles are obviously a decoy."

"Obviously," the Buddha repeated.

He coldly assessed me with his small piglike eyes.

"You're quite the Sherlock Holmes, aren't you?"

"He's nothing but a French has-been cop," Rafael said.

"Let's not dwell on the past, Rafael. After all, you were a Spanish cop before you got into cocaine."

While we were talking, the bundles were still being loaded onto the pickups. They had to be worth several million euros. Enough to make your head spin. I decided to switch over to the colonel, who was standing off to the side.

"Colonel, you'll be getting a call from Bamako soon. It'll be for me. When the call comes, please be kind enough to hand over your communications device."

"What? What does that mean?" the colonel asked. His eye twitched almost imperceptibly.

The Buddha pulled out a handkerchief and wiped the sweat off his forehead. "Explain to me, Mr. Camara, why I shouldn't kill you like a dog right here and now. No one will find your body and—"

The colonel's satellite phone started pinging. The Buddha rolled his eyes as the colonel answered, excusing himself. He gave the caller a bit of customary sucking up and then went white. He started protesting, claiming he didn't understand what he was being accused of. With a defeated look on his face, he shook his head. Finally he handed me the phone—a brand new Thuraya.

"It's for you," he muttered.

He signaled a guard to untie my hands. I grabbed the phone, my heart beating wildly.

"Yes?"

"Solo, are you all right?"

It was Hamidou Kansaye.

"For the time being, but I doubt that'll last."

"I wanted to make sure you were alive. Give the phone back to Doumbia."

"Who?"

"Doumbia, the National Guard commander."

I handed the phone back.

Next to me, the Buddha was fussing. "Can someone tell me what's going on?"

Doumbia was having a heated discussion with Kansaye. I was glad I wasn't in his place. But I wasn't particularly fond of the place I was in either. He ended the call at last, wiping the sweat off his face with the back of his hand. He signaled to one of his men.

"Lassana! Free him."

Rodrigo intervened before Rafael had time to stop him. "What? Are you crazy! This *cabrón* is going to rat us all out. We have to get rid of him."

The National Guard soldiers pointed their weapons at the Venezuelan. I could tell by their tense faces and nervous fingers that a simple gust of wind could set off a shootout. Rafael put a hand on his partner's arm.

"Rodrigo, please shut your mouth."

"This asshole-bitch is a protégé of the police commissioner," Doumbia said. "Who made it very clear that if anything happens to his boy, we'll pay for it. I don't want to get involved with the police."

The Buddha rolled his eyes.

Clearly, Rodrigo didn't know when to leave well enough alone. "So what? Why should we give a shit about the police commissioner? Shoot the fucker, and let's be done with it."

"You don't know Hamidou Kansaye. If we kill his protégé, my career is fucked, along with my business."

The guards stepped between me and the drug traffickers.

"We'll just buy him off, like the others," the Buddha said.

"We can't. This is his *boy*."

"He's his son?"

"Pretty much. If I kill him, Kansaye will be on us like a pit bull. He won't let go till we're dead. You got it?"

Rafael hadn't taken his eyes off me. I could tell he was thinking hard.

"Doumbia's right. Free him," he said, surrendering.

"What? You too, Rafael?" Rodrigo shouted.

"Shut it, Rodrigo!"

The Spaniard had taken the Buddha and Doumbia off to the side. I figured they were still weighing their options, but I couldn't tell what my odds were by the looks they were shooting me. The unloading operation was almost finished. The guys in tagelmusts were busy covering the precious cargo with canvas tarps. The pickup trucks' engines started revving. The drug lords wound up their chat and headed over to me. Doumbia signaled to one of his men to cut my ropes.

"We're going to let you go, Camara," Rafael said. "You can't do us much harm anyway."

"Are you sure about that?" I replied, massaging my sore wrists.

"You know very well that we've bought out this county, just like the other countries we've bought out. What can you do? Go cry behind the skirts of your Frenchies—the people who've been after you for years?"

I brushed the dust off my clothes, pulled my shoulders back, and planted my feet.

"You know I'm not going to give up till I get you."

"I know," he said with a smile.

42

I stumbled back to my car like a drunk after getting off so lightly. The pickup trucks and the three luxury Land Cruiser V8s had set off and were heading north. Beneath the oppressive sun, I went to retrieve my backpack from my lookout post, but not much was left. The soldiers had swiped my camera, satellite phone, and binoculars. I got in the SUV and started the engine. Along the road to Gao, I passed another convoy of pickups. I'd say Kountas, based on their clothes. They were probably planning to stock up on supplies from the Boeing's baggage hold, as the Algerian military men had before them. I wasn't surprised. The Kountas were involved in most of the region's large-scale trafficking—especially drugs. The Arab tribal group had thrown its support behind President Amadou Toumani Touré in his armed fight against the Tuareg Berbers. In exchange, Bamako closed it eyes. Once I was alone on the road I stopped to remove my memory card and cleaned it off. I arrived in Gao in the evening, exhausted by the ten-hour drive. Because the Malian guards hadn't rummaged through my vehicle, I still had my cell phone. I called Kansaye. For once he picked up on the first ring.

"Solo? Are you all right?"

"I'm fine, Commissioner, thanks to you."

Before I could say another word, he was shouting. I had to hold the phone away from my ear.

"What a stupid ass you are! What mess did you go and get yourself into this time?"

In the past, I had been able to calm him down fairly easily. This time, however, he wasn't going to be quickly placated. When I sensed that his blood pressure had dropped enough, I gave him a quick rundown of what had happened. He listened attentively.

"As soon as you get to Bamako, come see me," he said eventually, his voice sounding weary. "We shouldn't be talking about this on the phone."

He ended the call after I thanked him again. I parked in front of the Atlantide and was relieved that the hotel still had vacancies, despite the arrival of an Italian NGO that was supervising a well-drilling project. The transalpine volunteers had taken over the place, trumpeting through the hallways and causing a ruckus from one room to the next. Their carelessness made me wonder if the noisy toubabs knew just how much they were coveted prey in this region, where a Western hostage could be traded by al-Qaeda for hundreds of thousands of euros. I gave it no more thought and shut myself in my room without even stopping in the restaurant for something to eat. I took a quick shower, and still damp, I crawled into bed. I sank into a sweaty sleep, haunted by deafening chainsaws and gleaming machetes.

The next day, I had a quick breakfast and hit the road. I had rested up and was almost feeling good. Without a truck to track, I could give the desert's sweeping landscape my full attention. But a troubling feeling was nagging at me. It was a splinter in my serenity. I kept seeing Rafael's face with its quiet and persistent look of hatred as he freed me. The Spaniard had something up his sleeve, and in the days to come I would have to be vigilant. I drove all day and arrived in Mopti in the early evening. I decided to stay the night. I spent the rest of the afternoon meandering in the market on the Niger River. I slept at La Maison Rouge and got back on the road early the next morning. I drove the entire day and didn't reach the outskirts of Bamako until that night. My phone had service again, and I saw that I had missed calls from Pierre Diawara and Milo. The Serb was asking for an update, and Pierre had an update. Although I was exhausted, I called Pierre.

"Where are you, Solo?" he said.

"I'm arriving in Bamako."

"What were you doing?"

"Doesn't matter. Do you have news for me?"

"Yes. My kid, Yacouba, the taxi driver."

"I remember him."

"He found something for you."

"I'm coming now. Tell him to be there."

An hour later, I parked in front of the criminal investigations unit. Pierre was smoking a cigarette on the terrace. We embraced each other in the African style—forehead to forehead. After the customary preliminaries—he asked me how I was, and I asked him the same question—he waved to Yacouba, who was waiting on a bench, his eyes glued to his cell phone.

"You have something for me, Yacouba?" I asked.

"Yes, *Warakalan*," the young man said as he slipped his phone into a pocket. "I found the taxi driver, the one who drove the French woman that night. His name is Adama Samaké. He lives in Lafiabougou."

"Excellent work. You've earned the compensation I promised." I took out three ten-thousand-franc bills from my wallet and gave them to him.

He thanked me over and over and handed me a piece of paper with the address and phone number.

"I told him you wanted to speak with him. You can call him whenever you want."

I promised Yacouba that I'd use his services again. After he left, I had a beer with Pierre and went home.

43

"You have a gift." From behind his desk, the police commissioner was giving me a weary look.

"Thank you, sir."

"A gift for attracting trouble! You're like a lightning rod in a shit storm of problems."

"You know how unaffected I am by compliments, but now you're starting to embarrass me, sir."

He banged on the desk, making his papers fly and a jar of pens and pencils spill over. "That's enough sarcasm!"

I stayed quiet while Kansaye looked at me with rage.

"And enough with the 'sirs,'" he said, not quite as loud. "Do you know how many hassles you create for me?"

"I have a vague idea."

"A vague idea, eh?"

He got up and began pacing.

"Just this morning, the prime minister's chief of staff called me into his office. He bombarded me with questions about you."

"What does he have to do with this?"

"What do you think? Your little trip to the North upset a lot of people in Bamako. Powerful people. They're holding me accountable."

"So things have gotten to that point in this country."

"Don't be naïve," he said, sitting down again. "Your white side still overpowers your black side. You don't understand yet that countries can be bought. They've already bought Bissau and Conakry. It won't be long before they take Bamako and Dakar too. Everything's for sale here. And they've got a lot of money."

"I've got pictures—a cargo plane delivering several tons of cocaine."

"Who does that concern?"

"You, perhaps?"

He pretended to ignore the insinuation.

"You're deluding yourself, *Warakalan*. I am sitting on an ejection seat. One serious threat, and they'll heave me out of here. And you'll lose your last supporter in this damned country."

We were silent for several seconds.

"Want some tea?" he suddenly asked.

I nodded. The commissioner made a call on his intercom.

"The minister of the interior wants us to resolve your nationality problem," he said while we waited.

"My nationality problem? I don't understand." Actually, I understood perfectly.

"Stop playing dumb! If suspicion arises over your Malian citizenship, he could—"

"Send me back to France."

"Where you'd spend the rest of your life behind bars," Kansaye said. "That would relieve a lot of people in Bamako."

"Are those people actually that powerful?" I asked.

"Even more than that."

We drank our tea in silence, both of us immersed in our anxious thoughts.

Disheartened, I left Kansaye's office. I had rebuilt the semblance of a life here, but now I was facing the possibility of having to abandon it. I could leave Mali—I was sure of that—with no regrets. But there was no way I'd rot in some French prison, sharing a tiny cell with two other guys with stinky feet and stupid faces. Just picturing myself searching desperately for a corner of gray sky through a window with bars was enough to make me pack my bags and flee to another country where I'd never be found. I've always been allergic to prisons. When I was a cop working narcotics, I'd sometimes have to question an inmate. Every time, I'd try to get out of going, but I couldn't always find someone else to fill in for me. As soon as the guards closed the iron doors behind me, my stomach would start churning. All I wanted to do was claw my way out of there. No, I definitely wouldn't be going to the slammer. I'd die first.

44

On the street, I took out the small piece of paper with the number Yacouba had given me. I told the guy who answered that I was a businessman who needed a taxi driver for the rest of the day. He sounded hesitant. Most likely, he was doing the math. I quickly offered him twenty thousand CFA francs for five hours of work, enough to be appealing. It took him no time to accept. The guy asked for my location. I had been waiting a quarter of an hour when an old canary-yellow Renault 12 pulled up in front of me. The driver, a big Rasta with a pockmarked face and cardboard-stiff dreads, asked if I was, indeed, the person who had called. I got into the Renault. The driver started the car and slid his antique into the traffic.

"Where we going, boss?" he asked.

"Are you, in fact, Adama Samaké?"

The guy adjusted his rearview mirror and looked at me suspiciously. "Who are you?"

"Solo Camara. Yacouba gave me your name."

Samaké relaxed.

"That's right. I remember now. Yacou told me you wanted to ask a few questions about the little French woman..."

"Bahia Tebessi."

"That's it, Bahia! It's terrible, what happened to her, really terrible."

"Tell me what you know."

Samaké pulled onto a side street, where he could drive slowly and recall how the night had unfolded.

"A friend asked me to go pick her up at the police station."

"Stéphane Humbert."

He glanced at me through the rearview.

"You knew that?"

"Where did you take her?"

"Lafiabougou, to a big house near the hills."

Lafiabougou was a working-class neighborhood in northern Bamako, near the Mandingues hills.

"It seemed important. I told her she should avoid that area at night. But she insisted, and I dropped her off there. She couldn't stop crying the entire ride. It really upset me when I read in the paper that she—"

"Take me there, please."

Samaké sped off. Lost in my thoughts, I gazed through the dirty window at the streets of the big city, so full of wretched inertia and wonderful vitality. I felt a sort of ex-hilaration—me, a half-dead, half-alive man. As I headed toward my destination, a strange dizziness overtook me. I had the sensation of reaching the top of a roller coaster right before plummeting down the other side. I fiddled nervously with my chèche.

We were now in Lafiabougou. The sun had begun its descent, bathing both the makeshift stalls run by street peddlers and the more solidly built shops in a soft, hot light. Samaké drove until we reached a big cube-shaped villa just off Lafiabougou's main road. A tall wall made of what looked like reclaimed rubble surrounded the structure.

"This is it," he said, parking in front of the gate.

I got out of the taxi and gazed at the building, whose fortresslike appearance did not inspire confidence. I leaned in the window to give Samaké his instructions.

"Wait for me here."

The cab driver agreed and stuck a reggae cassette in the ancient Renault's dusty tape player. I walked toward the gate to the tune of Bob Marley's "No Woman, No Cry."

I walked in without knocking. The house appeared abandoned, but it wasn't. On the hunt for something—anything—that could confirm my developing theory about Bahia's slaying, I wandered the hallways and deserted rooms. I ended up in a large living room. They were there, waiting for me: two African guys, scrawny as stray cats, in filthy T-shirts and torn jeans. They were holding knives with long blades. They got up to welcome me. On the floor beneath their patched-up flip-flops was a huge dark stain. It looked like a brownish rug that the men had carelessly trampled.

"That's where you killed her," I said.

They didn't respond. They were flashing wide grins, their knives aimed at my chest. The bigger one made a move. His blade whipped the air inches from my throat. I dodged at the last second and drew the Glock from the back of my belt. Like a cowboy straight out of an old American movie, I shot from the hip. Two poppy-red spots of blood appeared on the guy's T-shirt as he collapsed. I was about to finish off the second guy when a blow to the back of my neck sent me to the ground. My weapon slid across the floor, out of range. It took me a second to regain my senses, my face buried in a thin layer of dust.

"Morons!" I heard someone shout. "I told you to be careful with the mongrel."

With a club in his hand, Samaké—my cab driver—was telling off the man who was still standing. The other one was on the floor next to me, bobbing his head weakly while bloody foam dribbled out of his mouth. He wouldn't be getting up any time soon.

"I'm starting to get sick of this shit," I said as I rose to my feet.

Samaké had picked up the blade belonging to the guy sharing the bed of dust with me.

"Oh yeah? Sick of what, exactly?" he asked, sniggering.

"Sick of getting clocked. Ever since this adventure began, everyone's been trying to kill me or smash my face in. It's tiring," I said, rubbing my injured neck.

Samaké was looking at my gleefully.

"I heard you'd be hard to kill, that you were a tough cookie, and all that…"

I was wobbling in front of him, too out of it to defend myself against what would come next. The reggae-loving taxi driver sank his weapon deep in my thigh. I shrieked like a madman as blade met bone. My eyes full of tears, I tumbled to the floor, holding my leg. Blood was already flooding my pants.

"I have to say it's easier than I thought it would be," Samaké continued. "Now I'm going to bleed you like a pig."

He leaned down and grabbed me by the ear, prepared to slit my throat. Like Bahia, I was going to end up in the river.

45

The tip of the blade pierced my throat, and adrenaline-fueled rage pushed me into action. I bellowed like a stubborn bull refusing the meat hook. I made a fist and punched Samaké in the crotch. Admittedly, he was in the ideal position for that, crouched above me with his pockmarked face. His eyes rolled back in his head like the reels of a slot machine. I would have found this hysterical if I hadn't been busy bleeding out. With his hands clasped between his legs, the cab driver fell on his back and let out an ear-splitting cry. His cohort rushed at me while I crawled toward my weapon, slipping on my own blood. I grabbed the Glock and flipped on my back. The hit man was hovering over me with his knife raised. I fired several rounds, riddling him with bullets. He fell on top of me blade-first, dead as a doorknob. A monstrous pain ripped through my gut.

I clenched my jaw and struggled to stay conscious. I was crying in agony as I pushed the guy off me. How could such a beanpole weigh so much? I stood up unsteadily. The knife fell to the floor, gunky with my blood. The room was spinning, or maybe I was imitating a whirling dervish. I couldn't tell. Taking hesitant steps I walked outside, into the fading late-afternoon light. As I stumbled onto the path, passersby gawked. No word could describe the pain I was experiencing. Incapable of taking another step, I stopped and opened my blood-soaked shirt to discover my innards hanging out. In a trancelike state, I held my insides and kept walking. Then, behind me, I heard the enraged man rushing toward me. I turned around. Samaké, holding the knife, was approaching me with eyes steaming with fury. Pedestrians had already started coming closer. I moaned as I leaned down to pick up a huge rock. Samaké slowed when he saw me brandishing my pathetic projectile.

"What do you plan on doing with that pebble, Camara?" he snickered.

"Throw it at your face," I croaked.

He approached with caution, pointing the knife at my stomach. I was still standing, thanks to God knows what miracle of will power.

"I was told to make you suffer before offing you," the killer said.

"Why'd you kill her, Samaké?" I asked, staggering.

"Why does it matter? For the money, actually. But I wasn't the one who killed the slut. If you want to know what really happened, you'll have your chance soon. You'll be joining her in no time."

I could feel my blood pouring down my leg and filling my shoe. I couldn't bear the agony of my shredded gut much longer, but I was determined to do something as long as I was standing.

"This man killed a young woman, and now he's going to kill me!" I shouted to those around me.

More and more people were edging closer.

Two things surprised me when I first came to Bamako. One was the speed at which a crowd could form. In a few seconds, a small pack had united around us. Kids, old people, workers, women…

"Look, he's still holding his knife. He's a killer!'"

Samaké, protesting vehemently, tried to hide his blade behind his back. "Don't listen to him. It's not true..."

But my call to action was gaining momentum.

"He ripped open my stomach!"

I opened my shaking hands to show the onlookers my gut, and a chorus of exclamations rose up. Like a single creature gifted with reason, the crowd began advancing toward Samaké.

The other thing that surprised me at the start of my extended stay in Mali was the way its citizens rendered justice without bothering with legalities. It was a merciless justice of the masses. With fear in his eyes, Samaké brandished his knife, yelling at the crowd to step aside. He tried to reach his cab, but someone felled him with a blow to the skull.

"Serves you right," I muttered.

And with that, the feeding frenzy began. The crowd rushed at him, pummeling him everywhere. He was disarmed in seconds. Samaké curled into a fetal position. As for me, I was writhing on the ground, clutching my gaping stomach. I felt weak. I was losing too much blood—way too much. At this rate, I would bleed out in a matter of minutes. As I wept, I untied my tagelmust and made a tourniquet around my thigh.

"Enforce Article 320!" I heard a woman yell.

Cries of joy met her proposal. Article 320—street code—came about during the 1991 uprising against the Moussa Traoré regime. Vigilantes opposed to his dictatorship took the law into their own hands by setting fire to their enemies. At the time, a liter of gas cost three hundred francs, and a box of matches cost twenty francs, hence the expression Article 320. It signified that the people were going to mete out justice in the quickest and most effective way possible.

In recent years, this custom had seen a resurgence among Malians who felt powerless against judges who were quick to sell their verdicts and police who padded their wages with extorted bribes. But Article 320 was also invoked against rapists, murderers, and the most violent thieves.

A man holding a small jerry can stepped up. The crowd parted and held its collective breath. Through my deep state of lethargy, I saw Samaké's pleading and swollen face. But that didn't thwart the guy with the jerry can as he poured its contents on the killer. The crowd moved back when he struck a match. Just before losing consciousness, I saw Samaké's body catch fire. His screams and those of the crowd were deafening. Children, meanwhile, skipped and danced in front of the blazing man.

46

The smell of burned flesh.
The smell of death.
The smell of shit.
The smell of detergent.
The piping-hot air, the gray drapes rippling gently at the window.
The light—white, blinding, brutal.
I blink. I want to call out, but my mouth is as dry as arid land. I faint with relief.

~ ~ ~

I come to in a soft and unfocused world. I don't feel any-thing except nausea and fatigue. And as I open my eyes, I see her leaning over me, surrounded by a white halo, a serious look on her beautiful face...
Farah.
She helps me sip something through a straw. I have the sensation of coming to life again. I want to hold her hand, brush her cheek. But then I sink into limbo, into my regrets.

I see her several more times, or maybe it's someone else. I see them too. Marion and Alexander. Alexander is playing in his room with his model Boeing 747, the one I brought back for him from New York. I had been working on a case with the FBI and had bought the plane at JFK because I didn't have time to go shopping. Sitting beside the bed, Marion is looking at me with a serious face. As always, she is worrying.

I sink into a pool of murky water.

~ ~ ~

Slowly, the pain returns.

I feel hot. I'm sweating, and my gut is burning. It hurts. It hurts so bad.

At night sometimes, I whine like a child. I bawl too, and the deafening sound of my voice hits me from far away.

~ ~ ~

I think I see Milo and Rony come in. Pierre too, but I'm not sure.

~ ~ ~

In one of those rare moments of consciousness or cognizant unconsciousness, I discern the presence of an old man sitting in a chair beside my bed. He is wearing a white Panama hat and has an ivory mustache and dark impenetrable eyes. He has a kind smile on his face and is holding a bouquet of fresh flowers. I sift long and hard in my clouded memory, but can't remember who he is.

He comes to visit me several times—at least I think he does.

~ ~ ~

"How are we doing today, Mr. Camara?"

I hated that doctor with the butt-ugly face and car-salesman smile. He asked the same question every morning.

"I'm okay, doc," I said wearily. "I'm okay."

He checked my chart.

Outside the open window I could hear the city quietly humming.

"All right, looks like we have a lower fever today. The antibiotics are working."

That way of talking like I wasn't there.

"When can we leave, doc?" I asked with a yawn.

He wagged his finger at me. "We must not be impatient." Then, just so he wouldn't look like a grouchy old school teacher, he gave me a wink.

I waited a few seconds and changed the subject.

"Doctor, when I got here, I had a blue tagelmust. I used it for a tourniquet. Do you know what happened to it?"

"Ask the nurses," he answered absentmindedly.

I sighed. Through the half-open door, I could see two police officers in civilian clothes keeping watch. The younger one waved at me. I wanted to respond, but it hurt too much.

~ ~ ~

Apparently I was lucky.

Samaké's blade had cut my femoral artery, and when I arrived at Gabriel Touré Hospital, I had almost bled out. Barely more than two liters of hemoglobin left inside... Without the tourniquet, I would have croaked. Remarkably, my stomach injury wasn't as serious. I was going to live, although I'd have to follow a strict diet for a while, the kind to make you regret having remained in this world.

In fact, I was damned lucky. I had survived the hemorrhage. The emergency room just happened to have enough of my blood type on hand when I arrived. I had survived the hospital too, and that was quite a feat. There were no complications during the operation to patch me up, no staph infection. And I got back my tagelmust, the one I had given Marion. It was all stiff with blood—hers and mine. That thing saved my life. But I didn't understand. Why had I chosen to live? Why was it that I hadn't embraced that whore, the grim reaper? Why was I always slipping out of her reach? I was tired of playing hide-and-seek with her. Doc acted like I should be thanking God for my miracle—for my resurrection. He said my sheer will to live had brought me through.

Jackass.

I wanted to leave, but I had to wait until my strength was restored and my insides—what was left of them—were healed.

Fuck, it was hot.

47

I walked like an old man. I thought the cane would give me the air of a sophisticated gent, but it just made me look sick. I had insisted on leaving early, and I was making my way out of the place. One month in the hospital was way too long. I couldn't take the captivity any longer. Initially, the doctors had refused to let me out, but I did what needed to be done. I paid off the nurses, and they signed the discharge papers. I signed documents too, but those were the papers stating that I wouldn't hold the hospital or the doctors responsible if anything happened. According to the doctors, I was only partially recovered. Milo and Rony had come to pick me up in the Land Cruiser. Getting into it was an ordeal. Milo kept making good-natured jokes, teasing me every time I yelped in pain, and despite my discomfort, I laughed. We all laughed. It felt so good I didn't even notice that I had ripped out two of my stitches.

Back at the house, Modibo was waiting for me. When he saw me get out of the Land Cruiser much thinner and barely able to walk, he cried his eyes out. He called the doctor to get me sewed back up. For good measure, the doc gave me a tongue wagging as he redid my stitches. I made faces, despite the disapproving looks from Modibo that said: "Boss, it's not right to make fun of a doctor!" Then, once we were alone again, the kid took care of me the way a son looks after his father. It almost didn't bother me.

~ ~ ~

I maneuvered on my three legs between the workbenches of the slaughterhouse. For some reason, there was an old coatrack in the middle of the room. I hadn't seen it on my last visit. I paused in front of the bench where poor Alejandro Nuñez had met his end—an end I myself had almost shared. In a way, I had been reborn on this abomination of crude wood, this birthing table crisscrossed with scars from the chainsaw. In fact, it was still there, on the table. The Malian investigators hadn't deemed it wise to take it. I brushed the chainsaw's metal housing with my fingers. The blade seemed to have been recently greased. I sighed and examined it. It was still pockmarked with rust. I raised my eyes and scanned the dilapidated structure. Sunlight was flooding through cracks in the walls, and airborne dust particles were dancing in the rays.

"Is this a pilgrimage?"

Behind me, I heard the dry and derisive words tinged with Spanish. The guy just loved to sneak up. I turned around with difficulty. Rafael and Rodrigo were standing in the entrance, blocking my way out. It didn't matter. I wasn't in any condition to make a speedy escape.

"You could say that. It took you long enough," I said as I lit a cigarillo, my cane dangling from my arm.

I watched them walk toward me, the butts of their guns sticking out of their pants. I inhaled the smoke, but it tasted like ashes—because of my medication, I figured. I threw the still-burning cigarillo on the filthy floor.

"We were expecting you, Camara. And it took you long enough to get out of the hospital."

"It's the starlet in me. I love to make a grand entrance."

The Spaniard almost smiled.

"So, you settled the score with Samaké."

"That wasn't me. It was this town that got him. I guess the vigilantes spoiled your plans. When we were up north, you let me go because you were going to hand me over to him."

Rafael chuckled. "All we had to do was wave our red cape in front of you."

"That's one of my weaknesses. I'm excitable."

I wasn't scared of Rafael or his buddy Rodrigo. I just wanted to get it over with. It was obvious he did too.

"Now we're closing the book," he said. "But there's still one thing I don't understand. Why the big vendetta? It's such a shame. We could have gotten on quite nicely, even worked together. After all, we're cut from the same cloth."

"No, that would have never happened," I replied. "You've forgotten about Drissa."

"Who's Drissa?"

"My caretaker, the man whose wrist your goons sliced."

"That old black guy? All this for him?"

"He was my best friend. Since you killed him, one of us will have to die. That's how it goes."

"And it looks like it'll be you."

With a smile on his elegant face, he aimed his gun at my head.

"I don't get you, Camara," he said. "You could have saved your skin by fleeing the country. You knew we'd find you if you stayed here. Why didn't you run?"

I was still looking at the table.

"Because this is my home," I said. "It took me a while to admit it."

Rodrigo had stepped around me and was eyeing me hungrily. "You should be happy then," he said, purring like a big tomcat. "You'll get to spend the rest of your life—the few minutes of it you have left—in your homeland."

"Too bad you'll never see your homeland again," I replied.

The Venezuelan gave me a confused look.

"What are you talking about, Camara?" Rafael asked.

"*He* thinks your traveling days are over," I said, pointing behind the two drug traffickers.

Still aiming their guns at me, they turned their heads to see who I was pointing at. An old man was, indeed, standing behind them. He was wearing a white linen suit, classic moccasins, and an off-white Panama hat. His handsome ivory mustache was a bit old-fashioned, and his eyes were as cold and dark as death. He looked like the vision I had when I was with the angels.

"Who is that?" Rafael asked.

"This is Tomas Nuñez, a rich and powerful farmer from Cauca Valley on the western side of Colombia."

"Don Nuñez!" Rafael shrieked. "What's he doing here?"

There was panic in the Spaniard's voice—a quiver that gave him away as much as the veil of droplets that covered his forehead. The old man took off his jacket without saying a word. He smoothed it carefully and hung it on the coatrack.

"When I found out that Mike Kedzia was actually Alejandro Hilario Nuñez, I set out to notify the one living relative he had left—his uncle, the gentleman you see here," I continued. "Finding him wasn't easy. I even had to ask the French police for help. Can you imagine, Rafael? The French police! But I had no choice. No one in Colombia would have known about Alejandro's death, because he had assumed a new identity in Mali."

Half a dozen of Nuñez's soldiers silently slipped into the slaughterhouse. They were heavily armed, mostly with Kalashnikovs, and quickly deployed themselves around the Spaniard and the Venezuelan. Rodrigo let out a desperate cry, twisting like a cornered animal. The *sicarios* quickly disarmed him. Rafael, meanwhile, was trying to keep his composure, but the blood had drained from his face. I planted myself in front of him and took the automatic pistol from his hand. He didn't resist, as if he'd lost his will. The soldiers bound their hands with zip ties.

"You see, Rafael, Don Nuñez lost his family in the many battles between the Cali and Medellín cartels. Pablo Escobar spared no one in those days. The only ones to escape were the young Alejandro and Tomas Nuñez. They were the sole survivors. And you killed one of them..."

Rafael spit on the floor. His eyes had regained all of their intensity.

"Your nephew was nothing but a *maricón*—a fag—Don Nuñez," he yelled at the old man, who was putting on a protective suit—the same suit that the Spaniard himself had worn when he was chopping up Alejandro.

Two of the *sicarios* pounced on Rafael—as he cried out like a fool—and dragged him to the workmen's bench. The old man's continued silence made my blood freeze, even though, in a way, he was the embodiment of fate's merciless justice. It was Newton's Law in its most basic form: for every action there's an equal and opposite reaction.

"That dirty faggot was ruining us!" Rafael shouted.

Tomas Nuñez picked up the chainsaw and started it with a powerful tug. The old man still had it in him—most likely thanks to his days in the fields. He leaned over Rafael, his power tool humming in his hand. I decided it was time to head out. I had seen enough butchery. Outside, the Harmattan winds were sweeping through the wild grass. I shielded the flame of my lighter and lit a cigarillo. Inside, the chainsaw was singing its head off.

48

To complete my investigation, all I had left to do was pay a visit to the protagonist in this case. I parked in the cargo area at Bamako-Sénou International Airport and went through security by paying off an Air Transport officer. On the tarmac, my cane sank into the hot asphalt. The sweat dripping down my back and under my armpits had a chemical smell, like the pills I had to take every day. I found Stéphane Humbert in the little office of his two-plane hangar. He was doing paperwork next to an air conditioner that was sending out a weak flow of tepid air.

"Mr. Camara?" he said, raising his head. "Are you hurt? What happened to you?"

I dismissed the question with a wave of my hand.

"Hello, Stéphane. I've come to tell you that Bahia Tebessi's murder has been solved."

He invited me to sit down. "I'm relieved to hear that, even though I'll always feel guilty. In a way, I'm responsible."

"In a way," I repeated, nodding.

Stéphane Humbert offered me a beer, which I happily accepted. He brought out two Flags from his little fridge and uncapped them. We drank the first few sips in silence.

I picked up the conversation again. "To be honest, I wanted to check out a few things you mentioned during our first meeting, primarily your little lovers romp in the Keyes region, near Sadiola."

Humbert smiled. "That was an amazing trip."

"To think how much better off you'd have been if you kept your mouth shut. By bringing up that little getaway, you pretty much handed over the key to my investigation."

"I don't understand," Humbert said, his eyes growing wider.

"I went to the site, and I made some interesting discoveries. That mine hasn't been worked in quite some time, and yet, according to Cartagena's website, it extracted gold ore valued at more than three hundred million dollars last year. You have to admit that raises some flags."

Humbert was silent. He looked worried.

"I imagine Bahia wondered why you were taking her to an inactive mine, a mine that was very productive, according to the company that owned it."

I took a sip of my nicely chilled beer.

"You underestimated Bahia," I continued. "She wasn't stupid. She was a law student. I imagine it didn't take her long to realize that the Cartagena mine was one gigantic machine for laundering the dirty money generated by the company's coke trafficking. I'm guessing our friends at Cartagena used part of their profits to make off-the-books purchases of gold ore from some other mine. Then they claimed the gold was extracted from their own mine."

Humbert nodded in agreement.

"When Bahia got out of jail, she called you. She most likely wanted to blackmail you and your employers."

Humbert let out a fatalistic sigh.

"She was very angry," he said. "She tried to contact me while she was being held. She wanted me to intervene, but

I didn't want to get involved. I played dead, and when she got out, she called me again, demanding to see me, or else she'd leak everything to the press—Cartagena, the mine, all of it. I was terrified. I thought Rafael and Rodrigo would kill me for being so careless."

My gut was killing me, and I was beginning to feel feverish. I took a pill while Stéphane Humbert watched me, his eyes full of anxiety.

"How did she die?" I asked wearily.

"I didn't want to tell Rafael and Rodrigo, but I figured I had to. Rafael sent me a thug—the worst out there. A guy named Samaké. I thought he was the one who was going to..."

He started sobbing, and the tears streamed down his face.

"But Rafael had decided that killing her was my job. He wanted to teach me a lesson. We went to get her when she was released, and we took her to the river, where the new bridge was being constructed. That's where..."

He was weeping like a baby, but I was incapable of feeling any pity. I had run out of sympathy cards.

"I couldn't do it," he continued. "I mean... It was too hard. I can't even kill a rabbit. So Samaké gave me a hand. It was horrible."

I couldn't take his crying any longer. I changed the subject.

"What's your role in this business of transporting the cocaine?"

He gave me a stunned look.

"You know about that?"

I nodded, telling him to go on with his explanation.

"I get permission for territory flyovers and handle administrative details—that kind of thing."

"Who else is involved in this?"

"Everyone, all the way to the highest levels of government."

His eyes suddenly filled with fear. "Rafael will kill me if he finds out I told you all of this."

"Don't worry about Rafael."

I took out my phone and entered a number.

"Who are you calling?"

"The police commissioner. He'll be taking care of you."

Humbert leaped to his feet and grabbed a monkey wrench. He brandished it as if he were planning to smash my skull.

"And what if I killed you right here and now? You're in no condition to resist. And then I could flee the country."

I gave him an annoyed look.

"Probably, but while I may be in no shape to fight, I'm still bigger than a rabbit. And as for fleeing, I hate to break it to you, but living on the run isn't so easy. Believe me. I've been there. You're not built for it, Stéphane. So sit back down and put that thing away before you hurt yourself."

The monkey wrench hit the concrete with a loud clonk.

49

She was waiting for me on the patio at my house. It was late afternoon, and Modibo had poured her some fresh orange juice. The crystal-clear ice cubes tinkled in the glass as she sipped the juice. She had decided to stay with me while I was recovering, and our living together was going pretty well. We were practically a couple. I eased myself into a chair next to her. She looked up from the paper, which she had been reading with a preoccupied look on her face.

"Does it still hurt that bad?" Farah asked, her voice full of concern.

"The pain reminds me how lucky I am."

She observed me skeptically. "I suppose it's all relative."

I glanced at the big headline on the front page: "Air Cocaine: Cargo jet stranded in desert leads to international drug-transport discovery."

Air Cocaine—you could always count on copy editors to drum up catchy headlines.

"I'm guessing the drugs the police found in Bahia's suitcase came from a plane like this one," Farah said.

"Probably," I replied softly. "Or from a trawler that goes along the coasts of Guinea, Senegal, and Mauritania. West Africa has become a hub for transporting coke to Europe."

Farah threw the paper on an empty wicker chair. I picked it up and read the article. According to the reporter, after the stash was unloaded, the pilot tried to turn the plane around and take off. That's probably when it got stuck in the sand. The dealers had no choice but to set the plane on fire and flee with the plane's crew in their SUVs.

"Where are you with your investigation?" Farah asked.

I put down the paper and looked at her. "I got the man who was responsible for Bahia's death."

Farah froze. She gave me a look that seemed to vacillate between relief and grief.

"Who was it?"

"Her boyfriend, the pilot."

I gave her a brief account, leaving out the part about the blackmail. I didn't want to do that to her.

"Did you kill him?" she finally asked.

"No, he's going to waste away in a Malian prison cell. Compared to that, a quick execution would be an act of kindness."

Her face hardened. "I wanted him to die," she said, enunciating each word. "I cannot stand the idea that he's alive while Bahia's rotting in a dark hole."

"He'll also be rotting in a dark hole, believe me. And besides, you know I don't do that."

"But you killed all those other people. Why not him?"

"Because I'm clinging to what's left of my humanity."

She had tears in her eyes. "The truth is, you don't love me enough to do it."

Farah had said those words like a judge delivering a sentence. She was already getting up and collecting her handbag. I didn't try to stop her. It would have been point-less. I took a sip of my Flag. The front door slammed.

"Maybe I loved you too much to do it," I muttered.

~ ~ ~

A few minutes later, Modibo came over in a panic.

"Boss! Why did she leave? She was very upset."

There was blame in his voice. He had fallen in love with Farah as soon as he laid eyes on her. Despite my many refusals, he had imagined her moving in with us for the long term. We would have been like one of those families in a fucking fairy tale.

"Put her things in a suitcase and have them taken to the Laïco Hotel," I said. "It's for the best, Modibo. There's a motherless kid in France who needs her."

He shook his head. I smiled at him.

"Go get me another beer and a soda for yourself."

When he came back with the drinks, I had to insist that he take the chair next to me. We sat there like that, admiring the spectacular sunset. The sun was sinking into the riverbed. It seemed to be drowning in a gleaming sheet of blood.

I sure do love a good sunset.

After a while Modibo got up to make us our dinner. I handed him my tagelmust. It was now more brown than blue.

"Could you wash this, please?"

The kid disappeared with the piece of cloth. A sweet jasmine scent was drifting through the air—the scent of Farah's perfume.

Against all odds, I was alive.

Thank you for reading White Leopard.

We invite you to share your thoughts and reactions on Goodreads and your favorite social media and retail platforms.

We appreciate your support.

About the Author

Laurent Guillaume is a multiple award-winning French writer and former police officer. In law enforcement, he worked anti-gang, narcotics, and financial crimes. He also served in Mali as advisor to the local police. He is now a full-time writer.

About the Translator

Sophie Weiner is a freelance translator and book publishing assistant from Baltimore, Maryland. After earning degrees in French from Bucknell University and New York University, Sophie went on to complete a master's in literary translation from the Sorbonne. She has translated a number of books for Le French Book.

About Le French Book

Le French Book is a New York–based publisher specializing in great reads from France. It came to be because, as founder Anne Trager says, "I couldn't stand it anymore. There are just too many good books not reaching a broader audience. There is a very vibrant, creative culture in France, and we want to get them out to more readers."

www.lefrenchbook.com

CPSIA information can be obtained at www.ICGtesting.com
Printed in the USA
BVOW05*1646151115

427222BV00012B/258/P